5/6/16

HAT

Please renew or return items by the date
shown on your receipt

www.hertsdirect.org/libraries

Renewals and   0300 123 4049
enquiries:

Textphone for hearing   0300 123 4041
or speech impaired

Hertfordshire

H0673642

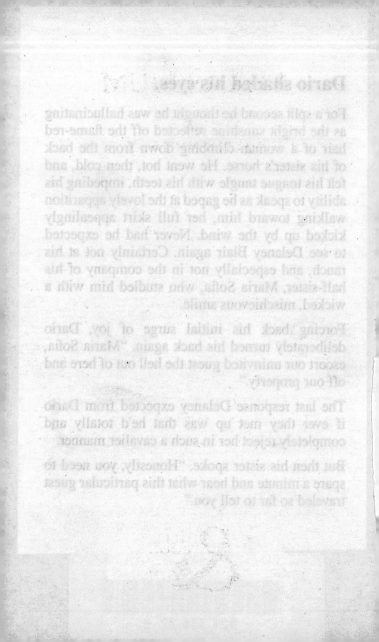

TEXAS MUM

BY
ROZ DENNY FOX

MILLS &
BOON

Published in Great Britain 2015
by Mills & Boon, an imprint of Harlequin (UK) Limited,
Eton House, 18-24 Paradise Road, Richmond, Surrey, TW9 1SR

© 2015 Rosaline Fox

ISBN: 978-0-263-25104-3

23-0115

Harlequin (UK) Limited's policy is to use papers that are natural, renewable and recyclable products and made from wood grown in sustainable forests. The logging and manufacturing processes conform to the legal environmental regulations of the country of origin.

Printed and bound in Spain
by CPI, Barcelona

Roz Denny Fox's first book was published by Mills & Boon in 1990. She writes for various Mills & Boon® lines and for special projects. Her books are published worldwide and in a number of languages. She's also written articles as well as online serials. Roz's warm home-and-family-focused love stories have been nominated for various industry awards, including the Romance Writers of America's RITA® Award, the Holt Medallion, the Golden Quill and others. Roz has been a member of the Romance Writers of America since 1987, and is currently a member of Tucson's Saguaro Romance Writers, where she has received the Barbara Award for outstanding chapter service. She's also a member of the Desert Rose RWA chapter in Phoenix, Midwest Fiction Writers of Minneapolis, San Angelo Texas Writers' Club and Novelists, Inc. In 2013 Roz received her fifty-book pin from Mills & Boon.

Readers can e-mail her through Facebook or at rdfox@cox.net.

This book is dedicated to all the devoted research
teams who work tirelessly to find cures for the many
forms of cancer that continue to plague us.
Time and dollars are making inroads.
I'm grateful for those who work in, march
for and donate to the cause.

Chapter One

Delaney Blair stood at the window in the hospital conference room. Lightning flashed as raindrops battered the glass. The summer storm sweeping through Lubbock matched her mood. Two of her son's doctors sat at the table she'd vacated. They'd been discussing Nickolas's prognosis, and it wasn't good.

Neal Avery, the pediatric oncologist who'd cared for Nickolas throughout his first illness, interrupted her chaotic thoughts. "Delaney, we've explored every avenue available to Nick at the moment. There simply are no marrow donor matches in the national donor bank. Nor have any emerged from the collection drives you and your friends ran."

Delaney rubbed at goose bumps on her arms and hunched her shoulders against the harsh reality of Dr. Avery's words.

Konrad Von Claus, a visiting pediatric oncologist and immunologist, chimed in. "I've gone over all of Nickolas's records from the leukemia he fought when he was eighteen months old. Like Dr. Avery and the others who treated him, I found no reason to suspect his remission wouldn't last. Regrettably, patients who fall out of remission require more aggressive measures." Switching gears, he said, "It's a fact ethnic minorities have difficulties finding matches. One reason is due to migration. Blood markers are inherited. Some families don't migrate together. And many people are from blended cultures. What about Nickolas's father, Ms. Blair? I don't see anyone named Sanchez listed among the people from your area donor drive."

Delaney turned from the window. "Dario Sanchez isn't relevant, Dr. Von Claus. He isn't now, and never has been in Nick's life. Dario lives in Argentina."

The visiting physician locked eyes with Delaney. "Hmm. I'd say he was a very crucial part of your son's life once, wouldn't you? We must face facts," he said a little more gently. "Among ten million people signed up to be bone marrow donors, less than ten percent are Latino. To complicate matters, Argentines are often of European descent. Their bloodlines are Spanish or Italian, but some have a mix of English, German, mestizo or indigenous. That essentially means Nick's chance for finding a match outside his family is well below the norm. We already know that you're not a match. For Nick's sake, you should ask his father and family to be tested."

Mouth twisted to one side, Delaney shook her head until her red curls danced. "I haven't seen Dario in over five years. Nick is four and a half…" She broke off and said, "Dario doesn't know he has a son. We met when my father, rest his soul, bought eight bulls from Estancia Sanchez. To make a long story short, my father died suddenly, the bank foreclosed on our ranch and forced Dario's family to take back their very expensive bulls and…the truth is he didn't care about me." Delaney's voice faltered again because the doctor didn't lower or soften his gaze. She threw up her hands. "You're right. This isn't about me or my feelings toward a man who promised to keep in touch but didn't. This is about saving Nick's life. I'd walk to hell and back for my son. I'll see if I can find a phone number for the *estancia* online."

Von Claus closed the medical chart and turned to his colleague. "You should go there and speak to Mr. Sanchez. Don't you agree, Neal? Facing someone makes it harder for them to decline. A phone call may make it too easy for a man you haven't spoken to in years, one unaware he's a dad, to simply cut you off."

Dr. Avery left his chair and took Delaney's icy hands. "Dr. Von Claus is right. Time isn't on our side. No man with half a backbone would refuse to help his own child. You need to see him and explain the whole problem. I know a trip will be costly, but I agree a physical meeting offers the best chance you and Nick have. You might also be able to obtain blood samples from his other relatives while you're there."

Delaney squared her shoulders. "The good people of La Mesa recently set up a fund for Nick and me. I could use that money to fly to Buenos Aires. But is it okay for me to leave Nick?"

Both doctors nodded. Neal Avery said, "Nickolas is here where he's getting the best care possible for his spiraling condition until a spot opens for him in Dr. Von Claus's study in San Antonio. We can arrange for Mr. Sanchez and his family to be tested at a hospital in Buenos Aires. Of course, if any of them are a match, that person will need to travel here for the harvest procedure."

"It makes no sense that I'm not the best match,"

Delaney said bitterly. "After all, I'm Nick's mother. It seems crazy to think strangers may provide what I can't. I carried him in my body for nine months." She fisted a hand against her belly for emphasis.

"I know," Dr. Avery sympathized.

"It is the best decision." Dr. Von Claus scooped up the thick folder. "It's good Dr. Avery suggested Nickolas for my study. There's much we have to learn about body cells relative to blood cancers. I've had cases where neither parent was a match, and yet we found a donor miles away with near perfect markers. If only storing a newborn's cord blood was a common practice, we wouldn't need this needle-in-a-haystack search."

"True. But who thinks when their baby is born, the picture of health, that any of this could happen? At the time, storing his cord blood seemed a needless expense. I hadn't built my practice yet, and I wasn't sure I could manage a baby and the long hours required to be a large animal veterinarian. Playing the if-only game won't make facing Nickolas's father easier."

"But you will go?"

"Yes," she said. The doctors said their goodbyes, and she turned back to stare out the window. Another flash of lightning cut jaggedly through an ugly sky. She stayed for an extra minute to settle her churning stomach before going to explain to Nick that she had to leave for a few days.

She finally headed to his room, trying not to worry about what she'd do if Dario refused to see her—or talk to her. And he might. She had fallen passionately in love with the dark-eyed, dark-haired Argentinian the summer after she'd aced her board exams and had been free of school for the first time in years. Back then, everything had been brighter, happier as she'd arrived home a brand-new vet. Dario and his crew had been in town delivering bulls and trying to make other contacts in Texas. If he hadn't disappeared a few weeks before her father's untimely death, their relationship might have been more than an eventful summer fling.

Too bad she had let her heart get involved.

Oh, what good did it do now to plow up old ground? She couldn't erase Dario from her mind even if she wanted to. Obviously the same wasn't true for him. He'd promised to keep in touch, then didn't. She was reminded of him daily, every time she looked at Nick. She only hoped Dario remembered her. It could be a death sentence for Nickolas if she was that forgettable.

Shaking off the gloom, she tiptoed into Nick's room on the pediatric cancer ward. His roommate had been discharged. The boy had been older, about seven, but the kids had been friendly. Today Nick looked small and alone in the too-big sterile room filled with monitors and medical trappings.

Breathing deep, Delaney bent over him and finger-combed the mop of dark curls off his pale forehead. His long lashes swept up, and he reached for her hand. "Mommy, where've you been?"

"Talking to Dr. Avery. Did you have a good lunch?"

Nick nodded. "But when can I go home? You and Miz Irene cook better," he said, referring to his long-time babysitter. "Here they always bring me bouncy red Jell-O." He crinkled his nose in a manner that acutely reminded Delaney of his father.

After Dario's disappearance, she'd made the choice to carry on alone. She had vowed her child would be a Blair. But when her beautiful baby boy was born with more of Dayo's features than hers, she'd made Blair his middle name and put Dario Sanchez as his father on his birth certificate. Her son didn't deserve to grow up with a blank spot in place of a dad. And mercy, weren't those Dario's big dark eyes imploring her now as she sat in the chair and leaned over to kiss Nick's lightly freckled nose, one of the few features he shared with her?

"Listen, my little cowboy, Mommy has to go out of town for a few days. You have to stay here so Dr. Avery can chase away that old fever that's made you feel so yucky."

His eyes glazed with tears, and he gripped her hand more tightly. "I don't like being here alone. Will Josh be back?"

Delaney stroked his hand. "Josh went home. I'll ask Nurse Pam if you'll be getting a new roommate soon. Okay?"

"Maybe Miz Irene can come be here while you're gone, like she does at our house."

"I wish she could, Nick. Unfortunately this hospital is too far away, and Irene still has to take care of Sara Beth so her mom can work. Dr. Avery needs you here, because they have the best medicine to make you better."

"I don't feel better. I'm real tired." He yawned as if to prove it.

"You take a nap, then. I don't have to go anywhere yet."

"When I wake up can I play a game on your 'puter?"

"You bet." Delaney dug his favorite stuffed cow out from under his covers and tucked his arm around it.

The toy had been given to him by Zoey Bannerman, the teenage daughter of a rancher Delaney worked for. Zoey's dad and stepmom had been so supportive throughout this latest ordeal of Nick's. All of the ranchers and townspeople in and around La Mesa, Texas had. Two neighboring vets were taking caring of her clients. The only thing the community hadn't been able to do was round up a bone marrow donor for Nick. And they'd tried.

She noticed his eyes had drifted closed and his fingers relaxed their hold on hers. She leaned back in the chair where she'd spent far too many hours. Firing up her laptop, she searched online for Estancia Sanchez. She hadn't visited their site in a while. Her palms began to sweat. Before, she'd been too busy making a living and building a home for her and Nick to spy on Dario—and that's what it felt like. Then their lives had been turned upside down when, at age one and a half, Nick had been diagnosed with acute lymphocytic leukemia. Living with dread, she'd juggled her work around doctor visits and treatments. The day Nick had been pronounced in remission gave the entire community reason to celebrate. And their lives were good until a few months ago when his fevers and unexplained leg aches had come back with a vengeance.

Delaney wasn't surprised to see a huge array of bulls on the Sanchez website. Bulls were, after all, the family business. The family sold them for stud and as trained bucking animals for rodeos. Her father, once head of the Southern Area Cattlemen's Association, had become a rodeo stockman. Some of his friends claimed he'd done so because of the prolonged drought—one of many things he hadn't bothered to discuss with her.

Wiping away tears, she scrolled through the website. The Spanish-style Sanchez compound looked beautiful. According to the information, the owner was Arturo Sanchez and his sons Vicente, Dario and Lorenzo. So Dario hadn't left the family business, although there was no indication how recently the website had been updated.

Closing the browser tab showing an image of grass-covered knolls dotted with grazing bulls, Delaney moved on to book a round-trip airline ticket leaving Texas the next morning. She also booked a moderately priced hotel in Buenos Aires. The total put a serious amount on a credit card she saved for emergencies. But this *was* an emergency, she thought, her heart melting as she gazed at her sleeping son.

She'd closed her laptop when staff wheeled a new patient into Nick's room. Delaney spoke quietly with his mother. Henry Nakamura, nearer Nick's age, also needed marrow and had fewer possible matches in the national donor bank than did Nick. Delaney promised herself that when they got through this and Nickolas was on the mend, she would devote her spare time to educating people, especially those of mixed race, of the dire need to be tested, hopefully to improve the terrible statistics.

THE NEXT MORNING she stopped to see Nick before heading to the airport. Parting from him took a toll on her heart.

"We'll spend extra time with him while you're gone," Nick's favorite nurse assured Delaney. "You just concentrate on what you have to do to get our little cowboy a donor."

Tears clogged Delaney's throat. All she could do was nod and swallow hard during her final wave to Nick. Pulling herself together, she dredged up a smile. "I'll phone you every day," she managed to remind him, pointing to the prepaid cell phone she'd brought him.

"'Kay, Mommy."

His breakfast arrived. Luckily for Delaney, her last glimpse of him showed him chatting with Henry about food.

Delaney couldn't relax on the cab ride to the airport or after she checked in. She'd brought veterinary journals to read on the long journey, but once the plane took off, her mind kept wandering. She continually reworded what she would say to Dario when she saw him.

Over eleven hours later when the flight attendant told everyone to prepare for descent into Buenos Aires, a major worry suddenly hit Delaney: What if Dario was out of the country delivering bulls? Oh, why hadn't she phoned Dario? That had been her first inclination.

Dawn was breaking. She rented a small SUV and checked into her hotel. She had managed scant little sleep on the flight. And yet, because she was anxious to put the meeting behind her and get back to Nickolas, she decided to sponge off, change and drive straight to the *estancia.*

Though it was fall in Texas, it was spring here in Argentina, on the other side of the equator. Most of the clothes she had taken to Lubbock were for cooler weather. Pride, though, had her opting for the one sundress she'd packed. Grabbing a cardigan, she made a face at the drawn woman in the mirror. There was nothing she could do about the plethora of freckles she'd never liked, or the dark circles under her eyes.

Delaney stopped at the front desk to ask a clerk for directions to Estancia Sanchez. She had only the address from the website.

Taking out a map and pen, the clerk drew a line that meandered through the city and out into what looked to Delaney like countryside. "I didn't realize the ranch was so far from the hotel," she murmured.

"It's actually nearer San Rafael. Depending on traffic, you should reach the estate in a couple of hours. It's a beautiful drive. Estancia Sanchez is *muy bonito*. The owners are well respected," the clerk said.

"Oh, do you know the family?" Delaney asked.

"I know of them. Many people mourned a few years ago when the patriarch was badly injured in a car accident that killed his wife. His second wife," she added after glancing around and lowering her voice.

Delaney blanched. "I...oh, I had no idea."

The clerk broke off speaking as she reached for a phone that had started ringing.

Mouthing a thank-you, Delaney clutched the map and hurried to her vehicle. As she wound through narrow city streets, the clerk's words loomed in her thoughts. She didn't want to feel sympathy for Dario. After all, her own father had died soon after Dario so callously ran out on her. Still, she spared a twinge of sorrow for him and his family. During their whirlwind romance, Dario had admitted that he hoped to leave the family bull trade. He had a university degree in environmental science and wanted to find a job in that field. She remembered his interest in the Texas weather patterns and water, or the prolonged lack thereof. He had been particularly passionate about the world's water shortage. But what he did with his life was no concern of hers. Water shortages, droughts and Dario Sanchez paled in comparison to Nick's problems. Her only reason for being here, for seeking out Dario, was to convince him to be tested for bone marrow compatibility with a son he had no idea he'd fathered.

Brother! Doing her best to focus on the gently rolling hills lush with spring grass instead, she at last rounded a bend that opened up to the grand vista the hotel clerk had mentioned. There she saw a wrought-iron arch proclaiming the compound beyond to be the Estancia Sanchez.

After she drove beneath the arch, Delaney realized that the entire estate was behind high, thick sand-colored adobe walls. She parked outside massive double wooden gates flanked by huge, intricately crafted carriage lamps. Alighting from her vehicle, she discovered the gates were locked tight. Noticing an intercom, she pressed a button. Nothing happened at first, then she heard the device crackle to life, and a man's deep voice growled something in Spanish.

Swallowing back a lump of anxiety, Delaney rose on her toes to speak directly into the box. "I'd like to see Dario. We met on one of his trips to Texas," she said lamely.

"It's Vicente speaking," he said. "Who are you? Please, state your business."

"I…uh…my name is Delaney Blair." She wasn't prepared for the vitriol spewed back at her in heavily accented English.

"You have some nerve coming here after all of the trouble you and your father caused my family during a time of crisis. You are not welcome. I suggest you leave now."

"What do you mean? I didn't cause trouble."

The intercom sputtered again, but the light blinked out.

"No, wait. You don't understand. I have to speak with Dario." Panic-stricken, Delaney pressed the button repeatedly, but to no avail. She doubled a fist and hit the intercom, but it really didn't help erase her frustration. Darn it, she had come too far to be thwarted by one of Dario's brothers. Vicente was obviously under some mistaken impression. Dario had left Texas by the time her own life had dissolved in a major crisis. And it was her father's lawyer and the bank who'd returned those bulls.

She stalked back to the SUV and glanced up and down the long wall. She could see the tops of some lacy trees inside. A colorful bird landed on a branch, trilling happily. The normalcy of that eased Delaney's fast-beating heart. Used to solving problems that arose in her life and vet practice, she wracked her brain for a solution. She eyed the wall, the trees and her SUV, and came up with a plan.

She backed the rental vehicle up to the wall opposite the tree and got out. Wishing she'd worn jeans rather than this silly sundress, she removed the cardigan and slipped off her sandals. Buckling her sandals to her belt, she boosted herself onto the hood and then up to the roof of the SUV. From there, she leaped to the top of the wall where she balanced precariously on her belly.

Taking a few moments to gather her breath and strength to propel herself into the tree branches, she caught the sound behind her of a rapidly approaching horse. Busted, Delaney teetered unsteadily as she swung around to see who had interrupted her breaking and entering. To her shock it was a pretty blonde woman seated atop a spirited palomino mare that danced and kicked up dust around the SUV.

"What are you doing?" The rider brought her mount right up to where Delaney dangled. "I'm Maria Sofia Sanchez," the young rider said, sounding imperious and oddly more British than Spanish. "You are headed for big trouble attempting to illegally enter my family's hacienda."

Tired, but determined to not look pitiful in front of any of Dario's relatives, Delaney dropped back to the roof of the SUV and wiped her hands on her dress. She looked down at the rider. The slender girl was as fair as Dario was dark. She wore gold hoop earrings nestled beneath a windblown mop of blond curls. Her boots and the mare's trappings screamed high-end. And the way she sat on her horse gave her the look of a reigning princess. But maybe she was approachable.

Delaney weighed her words carefully. "I buzzed the intercom to ask for Dario, but Vicente refused to open the gate. By the way, your horse is beautiful." Leaning down, Delaney stroked the palomino's velvety nose.

The rider said nothing, but she also rubbed her mount's golden neck.

Unhooking her shoes from her belt, Delaney slipped them on. "I'm Delaney Blair. It's been five years since I met Dario in Texas. I should have phoned before coming here, I suppose. But I wanted to surprise him."

"Oh, he'll be surprised all right. You're the American who broke my brother's heart and caused a huge rift in my family."

Laughing nervously, Delaney sat on her skirt and scooted to the front of the vehicle where she could more easily reach the ground. "I hardly broke his heart. He took off, never to be heard from again, and left mine in tatters."

The flash of sympathy in the horsewoman's chocolate-brown eyes made Delaney sigh and fess up. "Unfortunately Dario didn't only leave behind a broken-hearted woman, but a son who isn't well. Nickolas is why I'm here. He's what I need to talk to Dario about." It was clear to Delaney as she jumped to the ground that she had sent shock waves through the horsewoman.

"Did you tell Vicente that?" the girl demanded.

"No. He didn't give me a chance." Delaney slumped against the side of her vehicle.

"This is something Dayo needs to know," the girl said, shortening her grip on the skittish horse. "If you climb up behind me, I will take you to see him. He's out on the property. He has a crew banding a new crop of young bulls."

The offer was a gift. Delaney stepped on the SUV's running board, and, hiking up her sundress, she landed squarely on the palomino's broad hindquarters. No stranger to horses or riding, she gripped the ornately carved saddle cantle. Her host somehow managed to remotely open the heretofore locked gate.

"I'm ready," Delaney announced, and was glad she had a good hold, because Maria Sofia sent them rocketing into the walled compound.

The grounds were quite beautiful from what Delaney could see, with a profusion of flowers blooming around the sprawling home. She was then whisked toward rolling, grassy hills dotted with grazing bulls. Every so often the horse startled coveys of quail, which called out and darted across the hard-packed earth.

Settling the mare into a trot, the girl finally glanced back at Delaney. "You acted surprised to meet me. I wish I could see Texas. I guess there's no reason you'd know I'm the youngest Sanchez. I've only been home two weeks from schooling in London. I recently completed my lessons there," she added giving a shrug. "I'd rather have studied here instead of boarding, but Our Lady of Fatima was my mother's alma mater. Papa insisted I attend the same Catholic girls' school."

So that's why Maria Sofia spoke with a British accent. Delaney absorbed the girl's words. Dario's sister had unwittingly added another stumbling block Delaney hadn't considered before—Delaney was Protestant and Dario was Catholic. As if she needed another thing to stress about.

They were approaching a corral. Peering around Maria Sofia, Delaney saw a few men wrestling a young bull through a narrow chute. When the palomino pulled up short and crow-hopped to one side, Delaney got her first glimpse of Dario. Her heart rate shot up as she remembered—the very first time she'd seen him in Texas had also been from behind. He was just as gorgeous today. His mile-wide shoulders tapered to a skinny butt encased in low-slung, well-worn denim. He had a lazy way of walking toward a bull that defied description. Delaney felt her mouth go dry as her brain exploded in a...wow! There was no doubt but that Dario Sanchez was even more striking at thirty-one than he'd been at twenty-six.

Maria Sofia called out, "Dayo, stop what you're doing. I've brought you a visitor."

DARIO DIDN'T TURN at once. Instead, he calmly shot a tag through the ear of an unhappy bull that bellowed and kicked at him. As two helpers dragged the bull out of the corral through a side gate, Dario spun and aimed an irritated look at his little sister for disrupting his work.

The whole family had expected Maria Sofia's tomboy ways to be curtailed at her regimented girls' school. Obviously that hadn't gone as planned. Staring into the sun, Dario paused to blot sweat from his forehead with the back of one leather glove. "Look, Maria Sofia," he yelled, "how many times have we all told you not to ride wildly into a corral where we're working with bulls?" he said in a mix of English and Spanish.

"You're bringing in one bull at a time," she pointed out sweetly. "And this time I have good reason for making you take a break. Come, say hello to someone you haven't seen in quite a while." Reining her horse around, the girl directed her passenger to swing off the mare.

Dario shaded his eyes. For a split second he thought he was hallucinating as the bright sunshine reflected off the flame-red hair of a woman climbing down from the back of his sister's horse. He went hot, then cold, and felt his tongue tangle with his teeth, impeding his ability to speak as he gaped at the lovely apparition walking toward him, her full skirt appealingly kicked up by the wind. Never had he expected to see Delaney Blair again. Certainly not at the *estancia*, and especially not in the company of his half sister who studied him with a wicked, mischievous smile.

Forcing back his initial surge of joy, Dario deliberately turned his back again. "Julio, bring in another bull. Maria Sofia, please, escort our uninvited guest the hell out of here and off our property."

Chapter Two

The last response Delaney had expected from Dario if ever they met again was that he'd totally and completely reject her in such a cavalier manner. She numbly registered Maria Sofia recklessly propelling the horse between Dario and the chute where two wiry men were dragging in another bellowing bull. Through her misery, Delaney saw the girl garner Dario's attention.

"Honestly, you need to spare a minute and hear what Ms. Blair traveled so far to tell you."

Reaching up, Dario grasped the mare's soft leather hackamore, a bitless bridle favored by *vaqueros* to train horses. His sister had no fear and ignored most boundaries—it didn't matter how many times he and his brothers lectured Maria Sofia about the dangers for a slip of a girl breaking a range horse that stood fifteen hands high. Her mother, Dario's stepmother, had died in the accident that had maimed their father. From the moment she'd returned home from finishing school, she'd expected the predominantly male household to be lenient, Dario thought; even now she was openly challenging him.

He knew he shouldn't let his sister manipulate him,

but he gave in to curiosity. What possible reason could bring Delaney Blair to see him? Driven still by an anger he couldn't explain for a woman he'd never been able to forget, who haunted his dreams, Dario strode up to Delaney and asked curtly, "Okay, so what do you want?"

"For us to be civil, or is that too much to ask?" Delaney wanted to lash out at Dario but knew she shouldn't. An outburst would likely ruin her chance that he'd agree to be tested. She hated being reduced to dirt by his flint-hard eyes.

"It may be too much to ask," he ground out. "Especially since I doubt you've just happened to drop by to catch up for old time's sake."

Their sharp exchange had drawn the attention of the men who'd apparently decided to hold back the next bull. Changing tack, Delaney softened her tone. "I'm sorry I popped in on you without warning. I expected you'd be surprised, not hostile. Be that as it may, can we have a word alone?" She flashed a hesitant look at their audience.

Dario's first inclination was to refuse. But after glancing around, he saw how the others in the corral focused on them. Even Maria Sofia had dismounted and leaned toward them. Motioning for Delaney to follow, he turned and they walked toward the far fence.

Swallowing, Delaney whispered his name, her voice catching at the end.

"Just spit it out, Delaney."

She hesitated again, then quickened her step to come up beside him. He'd set a booted foot on the lowest rung of the wood-railed corral, flagrantly male and heart-stoppingly good-looking. The confident, sexy stance reminded her of their brief but passionate affair and drove Delaney's carefully crafted speech away. She couldn't control her thoughts. "You left me pregnant," she said and watched his body stiffen and his foot slip off the rail with a thud. She wanted to snatch back her words. Instead, she continued. "It's true. After you left Texas, I gave birth to your son. His name is Nickolas. Right now he's in a Lubbock hospital battling leukemia for the second time in his life."

Dario balled and un-balled his hands, yet said nothing, so Delaney talked faster, explaining how Nick had blessedly gone into remission after weeks of treatments during his first brush with the illness. "I assumed he was cured. Everyone did. But two months ago his fevers came back. He needs a bone marrow transplant. In a quirk of fate, I'm not a match. Nor is anyone currently in the national bone marrow registry. All of my friends and many of the people I work with as a vet have been tested. The problem is that kids with mixed blood present special difficulties. We need someone of Hispanic descent, and we've signed up and tested as many people as we can. I brought a packet of information if you'd like to study it. Or, you can go online." Delaney pursed her lips, wishing he would say something. "I wouldn't have bothered you, but Nick's doctors say he's out of options."

She couldn't bring herself to say to the stone-faced man staring so coldly at her that Nickolas might die without a match. Wishing she didn't feel so desperate, she wound down, continuing, "I'm here to ask you…beg you to be tested. The doctors in Texas can arrange for you to have blood drawn in Buenos Aires. You'd only need to fly to Texas if you are a match.

Even though I don't have the necessary blood markers, Nick's doctors think you or someone in your family might."

"This is all bullshit, Delaney. I don't know what you're trying to pull." He threw up a hand. "We only had one night together. But something I am sure of, I used protection that night. So your kid's not mine," he said, slapping his hand against his chest.

"I don't know what went wrong with our protection, but something did. You know very well you were my first, Dario. And there's been no one since. Not since you left me without a word."

"Don't pretend you don't know why I left. Your dad made it very clear when he caught me sneaking downstairs from your room at dawn. He ordered me to leave the ranch and to never contact you again, and he threatened to see that Estancia Sanchez never sold another bull to the Southwestern rodeo stockmen. Which he did anyway, by spreading lies about our bulls being diseased. We had a hell of a time regaining our reputation."

She stopped a moment. "Wh-what do you mean my dad ordered you to not contact me again, and held sway over stock contractors?" She drew back, narrowing her eyes.

"He said he'd spent a fortune on your education and you weren't going to throw away his dream of you being a veterinarian on some oversexed foreigner. He followed me as I rounded up my crew, making sure we left the ranch. He swore if I tried to reach you, Estancia Sanchez would never sell another bull in Texas or surrounding states. That's the bulk of our US business. I held up my end of the bargain, but he did all

he could to ruin us. On top of that, we had to eat the
cost of transporting home eight expensive bulls at a
terrible time for my family. It's only recently that Vicente was able to get anyone from the Southern rodeo
circuit to consider our animals. If you don't believe
me, ask your father."

Delaney massaged the suddenly icy skin of her
upper arms. "I can't ask him. The week after you left,
he was out on the range, miles from the house, and
his appendix ruptured. A neighbor saw buzzards cir-
cling late in the day and rode over to investigate. He
found my dad on the ground, his horse watching over
him. The medical examiner said gangrene had poured
through Dad's bloodstream, killing him. The weeks
that followed were the worst of my life. For one thing,
I had no idea he'd mortgaged the ranch to pay for my
schooling. The banker said that rather than sell off
land, Dad floated a second lien to buy the bulls. I
didn't even know Dad had become involved as a rodeo
stockman. The bank ordered the bulls to be returned to
you, not my dad. I had no home, no father and no practice to go with my new doctorate when what I thought
was the flu turned out to be morning sickness."

Dario's eyes widened. "If what you say is true, Delaney, I'm sorry."

"It is true. Every word," she said huffily.

"But why didn't you get hold of me then? Why
wait so long?"

"My God, Dario, you had dropped out of my life.
A woman has her pride."

"You wait years, then spring this kind of news on
me? Bah! So, who spread the word to other stockmen
that our bulls were flawed?"

"I've no clue. Maybe my dad didn't trust us, and called people anyway. He could see how badly I wanted to hear from you." Delaney's voice gave out.

Dario threw up his hands. "I tell you what, Delaney. Bring the boy to Buenos Aires. I'll arrange for our family physician to do DNA testing. If that proves my paternity, I'll undergo the other tests you want me to take."

Gazing into his unyielding eyes, Delaney didn't know where the kind, playful man she'd fallen in love with had gone. He could send off a swab to be tested. "You're an ass, Dario Sanchez. Nickolas is too sick to travel." Blinking back tears of frustration, she caught the eye of Dario's sister who had ridden closer, and she beckoned to the girl. "If Maria Sofia will take me back to where I left my rental vehicle, I'll go home and do all I can to increase the circle of potential donors. I'll cast a wider net in the Texas Latino community."

He met her glare for a moment, then shifted his gaze to the bull pens.

Maria Sofia barged between them on her horse. "Dayo, go to Texas to have the tests. I'll go with you. I'm bored here at the *estancia*," she said, tossing her long golden curls over one shoulder. "You all refuse to let me help with the business. While you're at the hospital, I'll explore Texas. We had a visiting professor from there, and I'd love to see the state. But Papa will never let me go unescorted."

"Stay out of this, Maria Sofia." Dario's exasperation was evident. He ran both hands over his hair. He began to speak, excluding Delaney as if she wasn't standing there. "Take Dr. Blair back to where you found her and get a phone number where she can be reached tonight.

When I decide on a course of action, if any, someone will contact her." He turned and walked away, dismissing Delaney completely as he called to the men lounging around the chute. "Bring in the next bull for tagging. *Ahora mismo!*"

Delaney's heart sank lower. She'd failed Nickolas. She didn't believe Dario would go through with the tests, but what more could she have said? Maybe she should have begged harder. Somehow she doubted if even crawling on her hands and knees to Dario would have made a dent. "He's angry at me for things I had no part in doing," Delaney said.

Maria Sofia stared after her brother. "This is so not like Dayo. Of all my brothers, he's always the most thoughtful and reasonable. Maybe he needs time. You shocked him," Maria Sofia said, gathering the reins and mounting her horse. She kicked out of one stirrup and offered her hand to Delaney to help her to swing up behind again.

"I suppose. I'm not sure how I would react if our positions were reversed," Delaney said, wanting to look back as the girl clucked to the palomino and they trotted off. But she didn't. Instead she wondered whether her father had gone to the lengths Dario claimed. Perhaps. He'd raised her alone from the age of three after her mother had drowned. She and Dario had loss in common. He'd told her his mother had died of a pulmonary embolism shortly after his youngest brother was born. And now his stepmother—killed in a car accident. They'd all suffered. She couldn't bear the thought of losing Nickolas.

IGNORING THE PAWING, snorting bull his two helpers dragged toward him, Dario tracked the retreating women. He wasn't proud of the way he'd acted. He should call them back. *Too late*. Distracted by the amount of leg Delaney was showing, he'd let them get too great a head start.

The bull lashed out, one of his back hooves grazing Dario's thigh. The handlers wrestled the animal into submission long enough for Dario to clip a brand pin through the bull's ear. The men rattled off apologies, asking Dario in Spanish if he needed to have his leg looked at.

He shook his head. In spite of limping, he motioned for them to bring in the next bull. As he waited for them, his mind wandered. *A son*. Had he really fathered a child? The very notion sent warmth curling through his chest.

It wasn't until he'd pinned three more bulls that he allowed himself to think about Delaney again. Five years had done nothing to dull the attributes he'd found so appealing when they'd met. Her red hair blazed like a wildfire. No less spunky, for sure, but maybe now she was thinner. He had noticed a change in her eyes. Still clear aqua in color, the bubbly spark had dimmed, replaced by a weariness he feared he'd had a part in causing. Undoubtedly he bore some blame. Maybe her dad hadn't told her he'd kicked them off his ranch. His own Papa would do that if he caught someone sneaking out of Maria Sofia's bedroom.

What a mess. Delaney's life had certainly been altered forever. Not just having borne a child alone, but dealing with the abrupt death of her father. He could sure relate to that. And if, as she'd indicated, Mr. Blair's demise had left her without the only home she'd ever known, well, it'd be a high hurdle to over-come. He had thought his family had weathered too much in the accident that took his stepmother's life and paralyzed his dad from the waist down. Always stalwart, strong and larger than life, Arturo Sanchez had been left crotchety and bitter. *Hell on wheels* was how Vicente put it. Add to that their business problems, and their family dynamics had been transformed, leaving all of them short-tempered. Maybe losing their share of the US bull market wasn't Delaney's fault. She'd acted surprised. Still, he couldn't bring himself to excuse the fact she'd waited five years to inform him he had a son—if indeed he did.

MARIA SOFIA RAISED her voice as she chattered nonstop on the ride back to Delaney's SUV. Much of her conversation blew away on the wind.

As she reined to a halt by the automobile, she said, "Instead of leaving and going back to Buenos Aires, you need to stay. I know, why don't you share our evening meal? If you like steak." She wrinkled her nose in apparent distaste. "Consuelo is an excellent cook. She always prepares enough for a half dozen guests."

"I can't barge in on a meal. It's clear I'm *persona non grata* with the bulk of your family," Delaney said with panic, as she dismounted and shook down her dress. "With luck I may be able to have the hotel concierge arrange an earlier flight back to Texas for me. I've hit a brick wall here. I shouldn't have come, but I had to take the chance, don't you see?"

Leaning out of the saddle, Maria Sofia squeezed Delaney's shoulder. "Don't give up hope. Have faith that Dayo will think this over and do the right thing."

The girl looked so earnest, Delaney's dispirited

heart gave one tiny lurch of hope. "I appreciate all you've done, Maria Sofia." She slipped out from under the girl's touch and opened her driver's door. Taking her purse out from under the seat, she dug out the ignition key and slid beneath the wheel.

"Wait," Maria Sofia called, dismounting in a leap. "Dayo said for me to get your phone number. And I'll give you mine so you can let me know if you're able to get a seat on an earlier flight." She tugged a phone from her jeans pocket and hit a few keys before turning an expectant gaze on Delaney.

Delaney rattled off a string of numbers, then retrieved her cell and keyed in Maria Sofia's contact information even though she was nowhere near as optimistic as Maria Sofia that Dario would have a change of heart. She managed a smile and a wave while sparing a last look at the walled *estancia* as she drove off.

DARIO LIMPED IN late to the evening meal. He'd finished tagging the entire crop of young bulls, separating out a good number to be made steers at a later date. He hadn't been surprised to find his leg turning purple where he'd been kicked by the bull. He was bloody where the sharp hoof had split his skin.

"You've kept us waiting almost fifteen minutes," Arturo Sanchez groused from his seat at the head of the large dining table. His wheelchair was within reach, but the family patriarch refused to remain in the chair at mealtimes.

"You didn't have to wait on me," Dario said, sitting next to Vicente. The whole family knew their father was a stickler for dinner being served at nine on the dot, as did most Argentinians.

Their cook, Consuelo Martinez, who'd been hired by Maria Sofia's mother, bustled into the room bearing a large metal platter filled with sizzling *bife de lomo*, sirloin steaks grilled to each man's preference. Arturo insisted his meat be *muy jugoso*—very rare. Vicente took his *jugoso*—not so rare. Dario and Lorenzo liked theirs *a punto*, or medium. Maria Sofia didn't like meat, and so Consuelo served her a crisp *ensalada* before she set the family-sized salad bowl in front of Arturo, along with a newly opened bottle of red wine. The old man tasted the wine, approved of it, then passed the bottle to Vicente to pour for the others. Each night, Arturo's sour expression showed his anger that the accident had left him unable to walk around the table to fill everyone else's glass. No one spoke until after their father offered up a short prayer to the Blessed Virgin. Since the accident, mealtime discussions had become restrained.

But this evening everyone quit eating when, seconds after the prayer, Dario picked up his glass of wine and casually announced, "I banded all the bulls today. Tomorrow Marcus and Jesus will start castrating the animals we culled out. Then I'll be going to America for a week or so to take care of some private business."

Maria Sofia clapped her hands and squealed. "I knew you'd do what's right. And I'm going with you, Dayo," she said in English.

Their father's head shot up, and his upper body stiffened. "What is this nonsense? You can't go anywhere during calving." His Spanish was precise.

Vicente let his fork clatter against his plate. "How did the woman find you? I ordered her to leave the property when she buzzed at the gate."

"Who buzzed?" their younger brother Lorenzo asked. "What woman? Are you holding out on us, Dayo?" he added with a laugh.

"It's the Blair woman from Texas," Vicente spat. "The one whose father screwed us over and cost us a bundle in money and prestige the month Papa had his accident."

"Oh. Her." Lorenzo scowled at Dario.

"I repeat, how did she find you?" Vicente sneered as he shoved aside his plate.

"I took her to see him," Maria Sofia said lightly. "She had good reason to be here. And Dayo has good reason to make this trip. Tell them," she said. "Papa, you won't let me sell bulls, so I'll go have a look at Texas."

Arturo pounded his fist on the table. "Enough," he roared. "There is nothing the Blair woman could possibly say or do to warrant Dario going to see her. If she's come sniffing around, she's probably discovered that you're now a full partner in the *estancia*, son. And Maria Sofia, you only just got home from London. You need to enroll in a dance class and volunteer at the museum. I already spoke to the curator on your behalf. We'll stop this talk and everyone will eat the flan Consuelo prepared."

Anger simmering, Dario wadded his napkin and dropped it his plate. For some reason he didn't like his family tearing into Delaney. "I don't recall asking permission to take a week off, Papa. I'm going, and my business with Dr. Blair is personal."

"I'll say," Maria Sofia purred. "Delaney Blair claims she has a four-year-old son, and Dayo's the boy's father."

Everyone's utensils clattered against their china. Stunned silence hung in the air. Suddenly, Arturo swore in rapid-fire Spanish, and Vicente and Lorenzo shouted questions in Spanglish—which wasn't uncommon as they frequently switched from one language to the other for business.

"Why now?" Vicente's voice rose above the others.

"I told you," Arturo snapped, "she's somehow learned that I divided the estate between you three boys, which makes Dario a wealthy catch."

"Stop it," Dario shouted, rising from his seat. "You're all bad-mouthing Delaney, and none of you know what you're talking about. None of you know her."

"I met her," Maria Sofia chimed in. "I think she's nice. Her son is sick. Dayo needs to take a test of some kind for him."

"A paternity test, I hope," Vicente said.

Dario glowered. "I'm not a fool. That's one thing I insisted on. All of you are no more shocked than I was. I thought it was impossible at first, but I need to know the truth. I'm going to do this," he finished, clutching the back of his chair.

"I took down her phone number," Maria Sofia said, holding up her cell phone. She scrolled through a list of numbers, stopped on one and offered the phone to Dario. "I can go along as your chaperone," she said cheekily. "To stop you in case you're tempted to take up where you two left off."

"Maria Sofia, you must start acting like a lady!" Arturo thundered.

Glaring at her, Dario snatched the phone out of her

hand and turned away, pressing the send icon, ignoring his brothers and father telling him to ignore Delaney.

BY TEN THAT NIGHT, Delaney gave up hope that she might hear from Dario.

While she'd waited, she had phoned Nickolas. He was such a perceptive kid. One of the first things he'd asked was, "Why are you sad, Mommy?" She'd tried to cover, telling him she was happy that she was coming home early and would see him the next day. She hadn't talked long after that, because of course she felt sad and her voice conveyed it.

She decided to pack so she'd be ready to check out at first light. She was half in the closet with clothes draped over her arm when her phone rang. Panic raced through her at the late hour, and her first thought was that something had happened to Nick. She dropped the clothes and raced to the bedside table. The number on her phone display wasn't from Texas, thank heaven. But her speeding heart didn't slow. Maybe it was the airline calling to say there was a change or worse, a cancellation of her flight.

"He...llo," she managed. Her hand shook so much she was in danger of dropping the phone.

"Did I wake you?" a deep male voice inquired.

Delaney heard an explosion of other men talking in the background, some in Spanish, some English. "Excuse me?"

"Delaney? Don't hang up. It's Dayo."

She gripped the phone more tightly, listening more closely to the background comments. Dario was catching heck from his family. She flinched when one man's derisive tone rose above the others in clear English, saying, "Dayo, you are a fool to drop everything and dance to the tune of a woman who didn't have the decency to tell you before this that you might be a father."

Delaney thought it sounded like Vicente, the man who'd answered the intercom.

A gruffer man broke in angrily in mixed language. "I'm ordering you to stay here, Dario. That woman hurt our family. Can't you see she's *la maliciosa*?"

Delaney didn't know the term, but she was willing to bet it wasn't good.

Dario shouted, masking the others. "I need a few days to wind down projects on the *estancia*, then I'll fly to Texas. You mentioned Lubbock. Is that where you're living now?"

"I'm staying near the hospital there. Nick is waiting for a slot to open up in a study in San Antonio. So you're really going to be tested?"

"First, I want DNA checked. Tell your doctor to order that. The next step depends on the results."

"It's an extra step, but okay, if that's what it takes," she said—but, what did he mean by seeing where to go from there? "DNA results take a week or more. A second cheek swab done at the same time would get you on the national registry. Why not do both?"

"Don't push me, Delaney. I'm getting enough flak from my family."

"I can hear that. But my concern is for Nickolas." She sighed. "Do you want to call me after you land, so I can come to the airport and pick you up?"

He hesitated several seconds, and Delaney thought he was going to hang up without answering. But he finally said a bit less curtly, "I'll arrange for a hotel cab at the airport. Give me the name of the hospital."

Tired and a bit sick at heart for the changes five years had wrought in the man she still had feelings for, Delaney gave Dario the information he had requested. He didn't say goodbye. She held her phone for quite a while, a range of emotions battering her. Some anger, yes, but more sorrow. When at last she put down the phone, her most fervent prayer was that he'd follow through on his travel plans.

It wasn't until she'd finished packing and had crawled into bed that Delaney began to suffer a new set of worries. While it stood to reason that Dario would be curious about Nickolas and would want to see him, how on earth would she introduce them? She had put off mentioning Dario to Nick. She couldn't very well say, "Hey, Nick, my little cowboy, this stranger barging into your room is your father." No, she couldn't say that. Even after DNA proved paternity, even if Dario went ahead with the blood screenings, even if luck was on their side—and that was a big if—when all was said and done Dario would return to his life in Argentina. She and Nickolas would go home to La Mesa. She couldn't risk letting Nick get his heart broken if he got attached.

She barely slept. Once she got on the plane, however, she convinced herself that all she could do was to face each hurdle as it came up. She needed to place all her hopes on Dario Sanchez being the perfect match.

Chapter Three

Delaney's flight home wasn't a nonstop. When she landed in Miami, she checked her messages and found she had a voice mail from Dr. Avery. Her body went icy, then hot, then icy again. Her steps faltered as she searched for a semiquiet spot to listen.

"I'm sorry to bother you on your trip, Delaney," the message started off. "Nickolas told me you would be home tonight. I have some information that will undoubtedly affect some of your plans. Dr. Von Claus contacted me with good news. His expansion grant was accepted. He wants Nickolas admitted in San Antonio, and he's arranged for a bed as soon as we can fly Nickolas down. We spoke at length, and I agree it's the best option for Nick. I took the liberty of lining up a medical flight for the two of you tomorrow afternoon. Of course it hinges on your approval."

In spite of the butterflies in her stomach, Delaney quickly called him back. "This is Delaney," she said when Dr. Avery answered.

"Goodness, are you back in town already?" he asked.

"No, I have a layover in Miami. Does this mean Nickolas won't need a marrow transplant after all?"

"No, no. He must have a marrow donor. But Dr. Von Claus's program has been successful in stimulating the patient's energy, which lets his team lower the frequency of radiation. All of that will hopefully give you more time to find a marrow donor."

"His father has reluctantly agreed to fly to Texas for blood tests."

"That's wonderful! I hadn't received any test requests. So, he's coming here, rather than being tested in Buenos Aires?"

"Yes, he wants DNA tests done first. It's infuriating and humiliating."

"I'm sorry, Delaney. Some men find it difficult to face hard truths."

"That's a nice way of saying he's being a jerk."

"Ah…well, it's a matter of opinion, I suppose. And you're entitled to your feelings. When is he arriving?"

"Dario needs a few days to wind up his business before he leaves Argentina. I'm not totally sure when he plans to get here."

"I'll alert Dr. Von Claus to prepare documents needed for all the tests. One thing in your favor, Delaney, with the larger facility in San Antonio, they have much greater access to labs. DNA results shouldn't take long."

"I guess that's something. You know I'm for anything that has a shred of promise to help Nick get better. Please, arrange the transfer, Dr. Avery. I'll sign authorizations tonight. It will be midnight or later, but I'll come straight to the hospital from the airport."

"I'll leave the necessary release forms with the ward clerk on Nick's floor." He gave her a bit more information about the receiving hospital, then said, "Delaney, don't be too hard on Nick's father. Remember we want his cooperation. The old saying is you catch more flies with honey than with vinegar."

"I know. I really do know that." It was just so disappointing that he didn't believe her. Didn't trust her. After she hung up, Delaney took several deep breaths. Then she scrolled to Maria Sofia's number. She should have gotten a number from Dario when he contacted her at the hotel, but she'd been so irritated by his attitude that she'd forgotten to ask.

The girl answered on the second ring, but their connection had static. "Maria Sofia, this is Delaney Blair."

"Are you still in Argentina?"

"No, I left Buenos Aires early this morning. I'm awaiting my connection in Miami. Could you give Dario a message? Nickolas's doctors will be moving him to San Antonio tomorrow." She gave the girl the name of the facility. "I hope Dario hasn't already booked a flight to Lubbock."

The connection was bad, but Delaney caught Maria Sofia's promise to let Dario know right away. "Our call is breaking up," Delaney said, plugging one ear and moving nearer to a window. "I'll be in Lubbock around midnight, Texas time, should Dario want to check anything else with me. Otherwise it's the same plan, just a different hospital in a different city. *Adios*."

She still had time to call Nickolas.

"Mommy, where are you? Last night you said you'd see me today." He sounded fretful. Delaney was racked with guilt for leaving him in the first place to go on a wild-goose chase. Although, if Dario turned out to be a match, it would be worth every minute of her time.

"I'm at the airport, honey. I'll be boarding a plane

soon, and that will bring me closer to you. Remember I told you last night I didn't get to only fly on one plane to get home. I'll see you tonight, but don't try to stay up, because you need your rest, and it'll be very late when I land. I'll wake you up and let you know I'm there. I promise."

"Did you buy me a present? Henry's daddy came to see him today and brought him a Dallas Cowboys shirt. I want one."

Delaney had been walking toward her gate, and it so happened there were gift shops galore. She checked her watch to make sure she had enough spare time to stop at one. "How about a Miami Dolphins shirt instead?" she asked, finding a table of kids' shirts on sale right inside the door.

"Okay, I guess. Mommy...Henry asked where my daddy works. I told him I don't got a daddy. He laughed and said everybody's got one."

Delaney's heart seized for a moment as she waited in line to pay. Was it Murphy's Law? Up to now she'd never needed to have this conversation with Nickolas. Henry was older than Nick, so it was understandable he might ask such questions.

"Nick, honey, Mama has to go board her plane. You be a good boy for the nurses, and I'll see you in a few hours, okay?"

"Okay. Bye."

She pocketed the phone, and paid for the shirt and tucked it into her carry-on. She'd never lied to Nick about the absence of his father. She had put off getting into it with him—waiting, she supposed, for when he went to school. Nick knew Zoey Bannerman had a dad, and yet he'd never asked her why he didn't have one. The subject had never come up before. Now it had. Boy, howdy, just what she didn't need—another problem to deal with.

More anxious than ever to get home, she forced her mind to things other than Nick's absentee father.

San Antonio would provide a whole new block of prospective Latino donors. If things didn't work out with Dario, she would need help arranging a recruitment event. She'd also need someone to drive her car to San Antonio, since she would fly with Nickolas. Maybe Jill Bannerman and Amanda Evers, her friends from La Mesa, would do that, and help her organize a campaign to register a new batch of prospective donors.

Her flight was called, temporarily stopping her planning. Delaney stood and gathered her things. Once boarded and settled, she got lost in thought again. It took a while, but she finally admitted she needed to feel as if she was doing something productive while she waited for Dario to be tested. Or with luck, maybe a stranger-donor would magically show up if she cast a wide enough net around San Antonio.

She tried to read one of her veterinary journals, but her mind skipped back to Dario, back to how good he had looked, back to how cold he had been. So, wouldn't it be the perfect retribution to find a stranger donor and be able to tell Dario she no longer needed him?

Or not.

Deep down Delaney couldn't help wishing he'd been someone she could lean on. Yes, she had done her best after he'd pulled his vanishing act to put him out of her mind. Of course he'd always lurked there.

And now that he was back in the flesh, gosh darn it, he was stuck there. Her heart had a far more charitable opinion of him than her head did.

A few hours later when her flight landed in Lubbock, she was bone weary and champing at the bit to see Nickolas. Delaney retrieved her bags and rummaged in her suitcase for a sweater to ward off a nip of fall in the air. Nick had taken ill in late May, and here it was almost October. Oh, how she hoped he wouldn't have to spend Halloween in the hospital. But that, too, was probably wishful thinking.

She arrived at the hospital after midnight. Per the hospital rules, she stopped at the main desk to check in. The night registrar knew her well, since she'd been there through Nick's first bout with cancer, too. "Is everything all right with your son, Dr. Blair?" the woman asked. "Or did you go out for a breath of air before I came on shift?"

"I've been out of town for a couple of days, Marge. I know Nick will be asleep, but I promised him I'd come in when my flight arrived. I'll probably spend the night at his bedside. Tomorrow he's being transferred to San Antonio."

The sympathetic clerk shot Delaney a look of concern.

"Nick's doctor says it's a positive move," she assured the woman. At this small hospital, staff became like family.

"Then, that's good," the woman said. "Would you like me to have an orderly prepare you a cot?"

"Thanks, but the chair reclines. I don't want to disturb his roommate."

A harried-looking man entered the hospital and

approached the desk, so Delaney waved and headed for the elevators. She rode up with a couple of tired-looking interns. They got off on the surgical floor. Delaney went up two more floors to the pediatric area, which split off into a variety of wings. She was all too familiar with the cancer ward.

At the nursing station she was again greeted like an old friend. One of Nick's favorite nurses, a young, dark-haired and cherry-cheeked woman, smiled and handed Delaney a folder. "Dr. Avery said you'd be by quite late. After you check on Nickolas, if you'd like to go to the waiting room, look these over and sign where the doctor put red *x*'s, we should be able to get his transfer scheduled for tomorrow afternoon. I hate to see him go, but professionally speaking, I hope they can help him make a full recovery."

"You and me both, Jessie." Delaney took the folder and tucked it under her arm. Glancing back, she said, "I'll probably spend what's left of the night. I'd appreciate it if someone can drop off a blanket."

The nurse nodded, and Delaney went down the hall. She peeked in, then entered Nick's room. She was always struck by how small he looked in the bed. One arm was hooked up to a hydration drip, and the other was curled tightly around his stuffed cow. She set the folder and her purse on the chair and riffled her fingers through his dark hair. Last time, chemo had left him nearly bald. This time they were using only radiation. It had other devastating effects, but he hadn't lost his hair.

Was it her imagination or were his eyelids more translucent and bruised-looking? He seemed thinner, if possible, from when she'd left him. The radiation gave him stomachaches, and on the days he had the treatments, he didn't eat. Was he wasting away before her eyes? Could Dario reverse it?

"Mommy?" Nickolas barely uttered the word, but his eyes, open now, looked large and dark in the soft glow of light that was always on behind the bed.

She leaned down and pressed a kiss to his forehead. "Shh. It's very late, and we don't want to disturb Henry."

Nodding, he touched her face. "Did you bring my football shirt?"

"I have it. You can see it in the morning when there's better light."

"Okay. Will you stay?"

"Yes. I have to go sign some papers for Dr. Avery, but I'll stay right here until after you go back to sleep. And I'll be here when you wake up in the morning."

He didn't respond but grasped her hand, forcing her to perch awkwardly on the edge of the recliner. She watched his incredibly long eyelashes as his eyes slowly drifted shut. She loved him so much. Her heart was a lump of lead in her chest. Nick was incredibly trusting, as if he believed her very presence could make him better. If only that were true.

Sitting in the semidarkness amid the clicks, hums and beeps of the equipment monitoring her child's vital signs, Delaney found herself praying that Dario would show up in San Antonio and his blood would be near enough a match to Nick's to give their son a chance for a full recovery. So many times of late she had bargained with God for Nick's life. She didn't know what she had to give in exchange, but she'd put everything on the table.

Delaney brushed his warm little fingers with her thumb until his hand relaxed and dropped away from hers. Only then did she take the folder and go down to the empty waiting area. As a rule there were always anxious parents or other family members there, sitting in quiet groups, drinking coffee from the large industrial pot. Tonight she didn't want coffee. But after reading the same paragraph several times without making sense of it, she rose and poured herself a cup. The aroma alone helped her digest the complicated content. She read to the end of the document, then sat and stared into space.

Her signature would permit Dr. Von Claus to place Nick in an experimental program where limited data suggested promise of beefing up his energy. As always there were risks. He might be allergic to the experimental cocktail of meds, for example.

Rising, she went to the sink and dumped what remained of her coffee. She remembered back to the boy her son had been after he'd gone into remission, before the fevers had returned with a vengeance. He'd been a normal, happy-go-lucky kid whose curiosity had seemed boundless. Now he was pale and wan, and intermittent fevers sapped his will to get out of bed.

Yawning, she paced around the table and massaged tight knots in her shoulders. If only she had family with whom to bat around the pros and cons of this offer. She hesitated to call it an opportunity, because all results from the study weren't rosy.

Did she trust Dr. Von Claus and Dr. Avery? Without answering her own question, she picked up a pen and scribbled her name beside the red *x*'s. As a veterinarian there were times she'd given advice based on her gut instinct and sketchy evidence. Closing the folder, she took it back to Nurse Jessie. Then she took the thin blanket the nurse had scrounged up and hurried back to Nick's room where she relaxed as best she could in the recliner.

A CRESCENT MOON and a few stars still adorned the lavender early morning sky when Dario exited the hacienda and tossed two suitcases into the back of his Range Rover. He was flying off to Texas, and he hadn't slept much over the past several nights. His ears still rang from the daily battles with his father and his older brother, who also thought he ruled the roost now. Lorenzo had bowed out of the squabbles shortly after Delaney's visit.

Dario thought about how much he disliked arguments, unlike the other hotheaded men in the Sanchez family. He'd tried to reason with them, then cajole them. He'd appealed to their sense of duty. Nothing swayed the old man or Vicente. During last night's fracas at dinner, his father had threatened to have Benito Molina, the *estancia* attorney, strike Dario's share in the hacienda and the business. Then Maria Sofia had waded in, demanding to know why she didn't get an equal share of the family holdings, which opened a whole other debate. The three sons knew, of course, that *su padre* believed women should be taken care of by their father, brothers or husbands. Their little sister had her own strong views on that.

Hoping he could put the whole mess behind him while in Texas, Dario fastened his seat belt and thrust the key into the ignition. All at once the rear passenger door opened, and he saw a bag or two tossed in before the door slammed and he was plunged into darkness. Then the front passenger door opened, and Maria Sofia climbed in.

"What in the devil are you doing?" Dario roared.

"Going to Texas with you," she said, settling into her seat. "We'd better hurry, or we could miss the flight."

"*We* are not going anywhere. You, Maria Sofia, are staying here."

She shook her head.

"Out." He shooed at her with his right hand. "You don't have a ticket, and even if I wanted to buy you one at the airport, even if there are spots available on both legs of my flight, Papa would skin us alive when we return."

She pulled some papers from her shoulder bag and waved them under his nose. "I have tickets, Dayo. Papa paid, but he had Lorenzo book online for me."

"Why? Why would Papa do that?"

"Drive, and I'll tell you."

Ribbons of sunlight had begun to lighten the sky overhead. Dario threw the Range Rover in gear. Only after they were through the gate did he ask, "So, did all of these big changes come about after I left the table last night?"

"Yes. Vicente would have no part of it. I could have done the booking myself. Papa is so provincial." She shot Dario a grin that he didn't return. "I think he caved because he's afraid you'll do something stupid, like marry Delaney Blair. And Lorenzo said, while I'm gone, Papa's going hunting for some suitable man to take me off his hands. He's near apoplectic at the thought of me wanting an equal share in the *estancia*."

She rolled her eyes. "Can you believe he still thinks arranged marriages are acceptable?"

Dario grunted and tightened his grip on the steering wheel.

"My mother would have never gone along with that idea."

"I don't know." Dario shrugged. "My mother would have fought him tooth and nail. She was a firebrand. Your mother was a lady in every sense of the word. She loved Papa and catered to his every whim."

"That's so lame. Well, I'm not going to be coerced into marriage. And you're a fine one to talk. You walk off instead of standing up to Papa and Vicente. I guess I can understand you taking heat from Papa. But what right does Vicente have to yell and get so angry at you for wanting to go see Delaney Blair?"

Dario shot her a veiled look. "Vicente loved someone when he wasn't much older than you are now. They were engaged, and planning a big wedding. Soledad begged to go with them when he and Papa delivered bulls to a rancher in Wyoming, and then she ran off with a rodeo bull rider. Vicente says he's over it, but he isn't. It's why he doesn't work with the bulls, never makes deliveries and instead only handles the financial end."

"How come I didn't know any of that?"

"You were a toddler. And Vicente remains bitter. He holds his loss against all Americans. That's why I didn't fight with him about Delaney. He's not going to change his mind."

"That's so unfair. Instead of holding a grudge, he should have found someone else to love."

"Mmm-hmm," Dario mumbled. They drove in silence as they entered the city and traffic picked up.

"I want to market our bulls," Maria Sofia said, veering to a side topic.

"You what? Now, wait a minute." Afraid of sounding too much like his father, he elected to bite back a remark hovering on the tip of his tongue, mainly that selling bulls was no job for a young woman.

"Would you stand up for me? Papa might listen to you."

"Maria Sofia, I don't think your years at a finicky girls' school lays the groundwork to sell cantankerous bulls."

"I don't, either, which is why I took online courses in marketing from a reputable university, too." She shot him a smile.

All he could do was laugh as he pulled the Range Rover into airport parking. "And that is something my mother would have done to outsmart my father. We'll talk about some of your ideas later. I'm sure we'll have downtime in San Antonio. Even if you convince me, you still have to get approval from Papa, Vicente and Lorenzo. We're all equal partners, remember."

"The fact you've said you'll listen gives me hope, Dayo. I got all A's in my marketing courses. The final paper I presented was based on our family operation. The professor said I showed ways to cut costs and increase sales by up to forty percent. I think money softens the hard heads of men like Vicente and Papa, don't you?"

"As someone who's still smarting from going three rounds with them and not winning, I'm in no position to offer help." He parked and pocketed his key. "Let's scramble. If the international check-in lines aren't too long, we may have time for coffee. Here, let me get your bags. Do you have your passport?"

She nudged him away from the passenger door and crossed her eyes deliberately. "Stop being such a Sanchez. I'm capable of carrying my own bags."

Dario drew back. "You don't always have to flex your muscle to gain respect."

"It seemed to me your respect for Delaney ticked up after she called you an ass and told all of us she was going back to Texas to find other donors."

Lengthening his stride, Dario didn't argue.

DELANEY FELT LOST in the larger city of San Antonio and in the bigger hospital. She was staying in a budget motel within walking distance of the hospital. It was noisy, but she thought it was safe.

Nick had become more fretful, too. Until he completed a full range of admitting examinations, he was in a private room. And the nurses, while competent, weren't like the friends he'd left behind in Lubbock.

There hadn't been any additional word from Dario, and that worried her.

Today was Saturday. Jill Bannerman was bringing Delaney's car to San Antonio. Their friend Amanda Evers had had to go to Utah to see her father, who had fallen and broken his hip. Jill had had to wait until her husband, Mack, freed himself up from duties at their ranch to follow his wife to San Antonio in their vehicle.

Delaney had promised to meet them in the lobby of the sprawling hospital. She jumped up when she saw them.

Jill hugged her. Mack, his teenage daughter, Zoey, and Zoey's best friend, Brandy, hung back.

"Can we see Nickolas?" Zoey asked. "Then Daddy's going to take Brandy and me for a boat ride on the River Walk while you and Jill make plans for another campaign to round up donors. Is Nickolas worse?" the girl added worriedly.

Delaney hugged everyone before she answered. "He's not worse, Zoey, but he's no better. Doctors here have developed a new mix of meds we hope will keep the cancer from ravaging his strength. He's been cranky since the move. Hopefully seeing you guys will add some sense of normalcy. Everything here is new and confusing to him. By the way, until they complete his initial tests, his visitors have to wear masks. You'll see a box of disposable ones clipped to his door. There's a trash bin outside to toss the used ones in when you leave."

Brandy pointed to the rows of seats in the lobby. "Mr. B said I should wait here while he and Zoey visit Nickolas. He doesn't know me as well as he knows Zoey. My mom said having so many visitors might be too much for him."

Delaney took a second look at the two teens, who suddenly seemed less like kids and more grown up. "There's a smaller waiting room on the fourth floor near Nick's room. It's quieter than here and has newer magazines. You can go up with Mack and Zoey and wait there. But, Brandy, he knows you well enough. I'm sure he'd love to see all of you. And you said you can't stay long."

"Is there a gift shop?" Zoey asked. "Dad said I could buy something for Nick here since, with homework and all, I didn't have time to get anything in La Mesa."

"Nick's favorite toy is the stuffed cow you gave him, Zoey. Save your money for the shops along the River Walk."

Mack Bannerman groaned. "Don't tell them about the shops. I only promised the boat ride and lunch at one of the cafés that overlook the river."

Jill, Mack's first love and now new wife, patted his arm. "You big phony, we talked about how much the girls could spend on clothes in those cool shops."

Chuckling, the handsome rancher bent and silenced his wife with a kiss. Delaney was glad that Mack had found such happiness, but she envied the loving relationship he and Jill had.

Jill playfully pushed her husband away. "You guys go see Nickolas. Do get him something from the gift shop. I need some time with Delaney. Touch base after you finish shopping with the girls on the River Walk. Then you can swing back and get me." She picked up a large leather bag at her feet. "We're going for coffee, and to discuss a plan for another donor drive."

Mack and the girls waved and headed off, and Delaney ushered Jill to the steps that led down half a floor to the hospital coffee shop.

Jill patted her ever-present camera bag. "If we put a photo on the recruitment flyer of you and Nickolas, strangers will imagine themselves in your shoes."

"I'll do whatever it takes to raise awareness in the Latino population here, but I also have to consider the cost. Printing a color flyer is considerably more expensive than a black-and-white text-only one like I used in La Mesa. I spent a small fortune on the trip to see Nick's father."

"But it resulted in him coming to be tested. That's good, right? In fact, maybe you should wait until you see if he's a match."

"I gave that a lot of thought." Delaney paused to fill two Styrofoam cups with coffee. She handed one to Jill and indicated where she could add cream and sugar.

Jill helped herself to a generous amount of both. Delaney, who drank her coffee black, led the way to a table for two tucked into a quiet corner.

Jill said as she sat, "I sense that you want to go ahead with this donor registry roundup. I don't want to pry, but are you afraid Nick's dad will back out? What is his name? I hate to keep referring to him as that guy."

Delaney circled the rim of the steaming cup with one forefinger. "His name is Dario. Dario Sanchez. His family and friends call him Dayo. I did, too, during our short summer…affair, I guess you'd call it." She frowned. "To be honest, Jill, I don't know if he'll back out." She couldn't hide her anguish from her friend seated across the small table. "Frankly I go back and forth between hoping he comes and that he'll be a match, to worrying about other ramifications if he does. He was so different from the man I remember. His family, except for his half sister, is rude and controlling. Another big worry that one of Nick's nurses in Lubbock brought up—what if Dario demands equal custody once he's satisfied Nick is his son?"

"Is that likely? I mean, you said he's involved with a family business in Argentina."

"He is. But ask Mack to verify how charming and

persuasive Dario can be. Mack bought a bull from him that summer, too. What nags me is the nurse was once married to a Latino. She said it's a cultural thing for the men to especially want custody of their boys."

"Heavens, you don't need that." Jill spun her cup a few times before taking another sip. "I never got to know my real father, and I'm a new stepmother myself. I can almost assure you that when Nick is older he'll want some kind of relationship with his birth father."

"Probably," Delaney admitted, hunching over her cup. "Until the other day he never asked about his father. Suddenly I'm faced with explaining." She rubbed a thumb between her eyebrows. "It could be I'm worrying for nothing, Jill. Like you said, the man does live half a world away. And he seems content with his current life, which doesn't include a son."

"Exactly. So let's hammer out details for this recruitment. Amanda will be home Tuesday. Mack thinks you should hold it on a Saturday when more people are off work. Since testing takes time, for Nick's sake, we should hold the event as soon as possible. I can take a photo now, go home and make up flyers. I'll do all of the work and keep the cost to a minimum. If I overnight them to you, will you be able to tack them up where possible donors will see them in advance of the event?"

"Thanks, Jill. I will."

"And you don't think next Saturday is too soon for you to secure a spot for us to hold a registration?"

"No. I'll phone the National Registry. The local chapter supplies forms, a technician and equipment from a blood and tissue center for cheek swabs."

"Okay. Let's go see Nick. I'll shoot some darling

photos that will tug at the hearts of any stranger. Then I'll treat you to a decent lunch. I think you've lost ten pounds from when I saw you treating a horse at Turkey Creek Ranch."

"Worry causes weight loss, but I don't recommend it as a diet technique."

Hoisting her camera bag, Jill linked arms with Delaney. "This area is home to Hispanic families who settled here before Texas became a state. If this event doesn't net you a donor, we'll do more until we find one."

Delaney was about to say she hoped Nickolas had the time for them to locate a donor, but her cell phone rang. She didn't recognize the number.

"Hello." She stopped on the steps that led up to the lobby. "Dario? You're already in the United States?" Her eyes locked with Jill's.

"Yes, Maria Sofia and I are in Dallas."

"Okay. My offer to pick you up at the San Antonio airport still stands."

She dropped back a step and put her head next to Jill's and held the phone out from her ear, so they could both hear her caller's response.

"I don't need transport," he said. "Our flight arrives at one. We'll rent a car and settle into our hotel, then drop by the hospital. I've decided I want to see Nickolas before I have any tests."

She bit her lip. "Uh, I can probably arrange that. If you don't scowl and frighten him, Dario."

Both women heard the phone go silent. Dario had hung up without saying goodbye.

Jill made a face. "I see what you mean about him not being the most congenial person. I wish we didn't have to get back to the ranch tonight, Delaney. I'd volunteer Mack to stay. At least to let the jerk know you have friends who care for you."

"That's okay. I doubt he'll come by the hospital today, but thanks for the thought. I find it interesting," she mused aloud, "that his sister is with him. I could swear that was not in his original plan."

"Maybe she's here as reinforcement. Remember, you're the parent in charge of Nick. If this Johnny-come-lately starts making too many demands, you can ask the hospital staff to restrict his access."

Delaney wondered about that as she dropped back a step. Now she regretted listing Dario on Nick's birth certificate. Moving to let people pass them on the stairs, she felt her stomach began to churn. Possibly from drinking coffee on an empty stomach. Possibly from the pressure she felt knowing she'd soon be facilitating a meeting between Nick and his father.

Chapter Four

The women took the elevator upstairs. They donned the requisite masks before stepping into Nick's room. Inside, Delaney saw Nick sitting up in bed assembling toys on his tray table.

"Mommy!" he greeted her. "Come see what Zoey and Brandy brought me." He waved what looked like a plastic horse. "Zoey said it's a farm-in-a-bag. See, the bag unzips and turns into a barn."

Delaney thought Nick looked too pale, but he sounded perkier than he had since the move. Her own well-being always improved when he seemed better. "Isn't this clever?" she said. "Nick, I love how you used the plastic fencing to make a corral. Wow, there are horses, cows, cowboys and even a dog. Neat."

"And chickens, Mommy, like we saw that time I got to go with you to where Zoey lives. I wish I could go there again," the boy lamented.

"Nick, you remember Ms. Jill, Zoey's stepmother? What should he call you?" she asked, deferring to Jill. "He calls his babysitter Ms. Irene."

"Ms. Jill is good." She took out her camera and a light meter.

"What's a stepmother?" Nickolas asked, his gaze

tracking Jill's movements around his bed as she held up the light meter before adjusting her camera lens.

"Ms. Jill married Zoey's dad, Mack," Delaney said. "You know Zoey's mom died when Zoey was a baby. The step part just means Ms. Jill isn't Zoey's birth mother, honey."

His eyes widened, and even though he fiddled with the horse on his tray, he continued to stare at Jill, who was setting up her tripod. Suddenly he said, "But my daddy didn't die, right, Mommy?" Nick's lips quivered.

Giving an uncomfortable shrug, Delaney met Jill's questioning glance with a guilty one of her own over her mask. "No, Nickolas, your father's not dead," she mumbled, quickly adding, "Nick…Ms. Jill is going to take some pictures of us. So, we need to do what she says."

"Why?"

"We're going to make up a flyer with our photos, and I'll post them out in the city where people will see us and read about how we need them to have tests. Because you need bone marrow. A cheek swab tells if someone has what you need, then they get a blood test."

"I don't like my blood to get tested. It hurts."

"I know." Delaney sat on the side of his bed and finger-combed dark hair off his sweaty forehead. She prayed that one day soon his ever-present fever would be gone for good.

"Hold that pose, Nickolas," Jill said from the end of the bed. "Look up at your mom. And, Delaney, slip off your mask for a moment, and leave his hair alone."

The boy flashed Jill a tiny smile. "Yeah. Tell her to stop."

"I like messing up your beautiful hair. The last time you were sick they gave you a medicine that made it all fall out."

"Is that why Henry didn't have none? Mommy, can he come to this hospital? I don't like not having a friend in my room."

"Henry probably has to stay in Lubbock, honey. But as soon as they finish checking all of your tests here, they plan to move you in with other kids."

"Yay." He smiled again, touching Delaney so that she leaned down and kissed his hair.

He made a face at that, and Jill clicked one frame after another. "Those are going to be great photos," she said, straightening and pausing to cap her lens. Her phone played a catchy tune. She stored her camera and took the call. "Zoey, hi. I think Delaney and I have finished our business, but we were going to lunch. Don't tell me you and Brandy are bored with shopping already."

Delaney waved at her. "Don't worry about us going to lunch."

Jill laughed. "Oh, your dad's worn out? Okay, where are you? I'll grab a cab and come give your poor old pop a break." She listened and nodded a few times.

"Can Zoey come back?" Nick asked his mom in a loud whisper.

"Not today, Nick. They need to drive back to La Mesa. Maybe Zoey'll come along when Ms. Jill and Ms. Amanda help me with the donor registration."

"Okay," he said resignedly, and began shuffling the barn animals around on his tray table.

"Nick, I'm going to go downstairs with Ms. Jill to help her get a cab. Do you want me to stop at the nursing station and remind them it's time for your snack?"

"Unless it's Jell-O. I don't want that."

"I'll tell them," Delaney promised, following Jill out the door.

"I thought most kids liked Jell-O," Jill murmured, stripping off her mask and depositing it in the trash.

"I think Nick equates it with hospitals. They serve it to kids a lot."

"I noticed he's really serious, and you talk to him like he's an adult. Is that just how he is?"

"When he's feeling well, he's a regular, rambunctious boy. I do hold some stuff back. I don't want him to worry."

Stopping at the nursing desk, Delaney asked an aide if Nick could have a Popsicle for his snack.

The young woman in the pink uniform went back to the refrigerator and said to Delaney, "We have orange or grape. Will he like either of those?"

"Either, and thanks." Delaney gave Nick's room number, then got on the elevator with Jill.

Downstairs, they walked outside. Jill called a cab service on her smart phone and told the dispatcher, "I'll wait at the entrance."

Delaney's phone chimed. She pulled it out of her jeans pocket, saw the number and said, "Uh-oh, it's Dario again. I wonder if they missed their flight."

Jill appeared concerned as Delaney answered the call.

"Delaney? Dayo. We're in San Antonio. Maria Sofia and I have checked into our hotel." He named one of the larger, nicer chains. "Did you arrange for the tests?"

Delaney flashed Jill an anxious expression. "For you *and* Maria Sofia?"

"No, only me."

"Dr. Von Claus will have to call in an order. I thought you said you wanted to see Nickolas first?"

"Yes, but I can do both today, right? Are you at the hospital?"

"Today?" Jill paused. "What time? I'll meet you at the front desk in the hospital lobby. In Lubbock I could have told desk clerks to expect you. This is a much bigger facility, and they have tighter security."

"I can be there in half an hour."

"So soon?" Delaney hated that her voice sounded unsteady, but her emotions were so chaotic when it came to Dario meeting Nick. Clearing her throat, she smoothed it out. "Fine. I assumed you'd want to unwind after your long flight."

"I don't see any sense wasting time. See you in half an hour. Goodbye."

"Ah…bye." She closed her phone and put it away. "Still abrupt, but at least he didn't just hang up like he did the last time we spoke," she told Jill.

"Darn, do you want me to stay till he gets here? I can cancel the cab and call Mack. He'll understand."

"Thanks, but don't disappoint the girls. I knew I'd have to deal with this sooner or later."

"Delaney, just a question. How will you introduce him to Nickolas?"

"I presume with his name."

"Maybe you need to just say, this is your father."

Delaney stifled a gasp. "Dario Sanchez is a stranger.

He'll remain that, since I doubt he plans to stick around, or even keep in touch. I mean…why would he?"

"Since this came up earlier I've been thinking you should prepare yourself in case he decides he wants Nick to know the truth ASAP."

"Nick is *my* son."

"And his." Jill impulsively hugged Delaney. "There's my cab. Listen, I didn't bring that up to scare you. But Mack mentioned that you never filed in a court to legally retain sole custody of Nick."

"Because Dario was never in our lives. He abandoned me, Jill. If he'd ever checked in, I would have told him I was pregnant. Lawyers are expensive. I barely kept myself and a baby afloat while I built my vet practice."

"A family court judge would take that into consideration. Knowing what I know from my own past, and from Mack's legal hassles with Zoey's grandparents, this may be a conversation you should have with Dario today. At the very least ask his long-term intentions."

Delaney nodded absently, but her stomach curdled at the very notion.

The cabbie stepped out and opened the back door for Jill. She slid partially in, but kept the door open, calling to Delaney, "Good luck. Let me know how the visit goes. I'll get your photo flyers printed and shipped to you."

"Thanks for everything. You probably think I'm terrible, or naïve, Jill. Before Nick's remission imploded, Dario showing up in our lives was too remote to consider. I mean…for five years he was nothing but a memory. And now I can't worry about anything except doing all that's necessary to find Nickolas a viable marrow donor."

"Of course." Jill told the driver where she wanted to go, waved again and shut her door.

Delaney watched the cab pull into traffic. She closed her eyes and rubbed at a kink in her neck. She wanted to take her son someplace where he'd be well and safe from all the things that weighed on her shoulders. Of course that wasn't possible. She had to see this through for Nick's sake.

She went back inside to wait for Dario and Maria Sofia, sitting near the entrance. She didn't have to wait long. She saw Dario walking up the circular walkway and took a few moments to compose herself. Rising, she crossed the blue-and-gray carpet to meet him at the double glass doors.

"Hello, Dario. Is Maria Sofia parking your car?" Delaney craned her neck to peer behind him, searching for his sister.

"I came alone. I wasn't sure how many visitors would be allowed at one time. And Maria Sofia thought the hotel pool looked inviting." The left side of his mouth twitched in a half smile. "Actually we had a tug-of-war over her coming, which I won. I… uh…wanted to see the boy alone on my first visit."

Delaney found that worrisome given Jill's earlier warning. "Nickolas. He has a name, Dario." She stepped aside for a group exiting the hospital, and Dario did the same. "Can we sit a moment and talk?" she asked, pointing to an empty row of theater-style seats.

"Sure." He gestured with a foot-long box that had a picture on the side of a fire truck. "I brought a gift.

I hope that's all right. I hated to come empty-handed. I saw this in the window of our hotel gift shop. If he's too ill to have toys, I'll run and put it in the car."

"That's thoughtful of you," she murmured, surprised that Dario sounded nervous. "Nick will love it. As I said, this is a recurrence. He suffers joint pain, erratic fevers and swollen lymph glands that keep him confined. He gets bored, and it's worse in this hospital, because until they complete his admission tests, he's in a room by himself. In Lubbock he had a roommate."

"Oh, I wasn't sure since you said he'd been moved here into a controlled program."

They paused in uncomfortable silence, but Delaney had to ask, "Pardon me for saying so, but in Argentina you were hostile. Why such an about-face?"

"Can you blame me? Seeing you after such a long time was a major shock. Your news left me reeling. Once I got past the initial impact, I did some research online about leukemia. I know so little. I couldn't believe how low the donor rate in America is for people of Latin descent. One article said a difference as great as eighty percent to four percent."

"That's Nick's problem. And it may not be as simple as our blood, Dario. Either of us could have ancestors of more than one ethnic group. But that's not the situation I want us to discuss before you visit Nickolas. Up to now I'd never had a reason to mention that he has a father. For now I want to keep it that way."

Dario seemed taken aback and said dryly, "Does he think you found him in a cabbage patch?"

"He's four, Dario. Because he was so ill at two, I kept him out of day care and preschool. I've always had a sitter caring for him at my house. The other child

Texas Mom

she watches, her mom is also single. I worked a lot of
weekends, too. He didn't have a lot of access to other
kids. It never occurred to him that he should have a
father. Frankly I see no reason to muck around trying
to explain our situation."

"How do you propose to introduce me?" Dario
frowned.

"If he asks, say you're an old friend of mine. Someone I knew before he was born. It's all true."

"It is, but it seems disingenuous."

"You know what, Dario? Everything I thought was
important took a hit when Nick was diagnosed with
leukemia. Circumstances surrounding our lives, yours
and mine…they don't matter right now. You live on
another continent. You made it clear you need to see
DNA proof that he's your son. He's a little boy living
in a restricted environment. But his former roommate
had a dad and he's begun to ask questions. I won't have
him hurt by a sperm donor flitting through his life."

Dario shifted his stance, and his jaw flexed. "I can't
make any promises to you or the boy beyond undergo-
ing the paternity test."

"Fine." Delaney hoped she didn't show her disappointment—or her fear that Dario might demand
greater involvement in Nick's life. Abruptly, she stood.
"If we're square on this visit, we should go on up to
the room."

Slower to rise, Dario lengthened his stride to catch
up. "Prepare me for what to expect. Is he attached to
tubes and such? Has he lost his hair?"

Stabbing the elevator button, Delaney glanced back.
She was surprised to see how nervous and pale Dario
looked. "He had all of that his first round with the dis-

ease. He went through a lot of bad stuff like a bunch of spinal taps and chemotherapy, plus radiation. He lost all of his hair, but he went into remission and his hair grew back."

The elevator door opened and they got in and rode up to the floor Delaney punched.

After they exited the car and she directed him toward the wing, she murmured, "They don't like to do a second round of chemo so soon after ending the first. Right now he's on radiation via pills. They sap his energy and upset his stomach. This study is designed to pump up his energy. But if we don't find a marrow donor soon, his doctor will seek admission for him to St. Jude's cancer hospital for kids in Memphis, Tennessee. That's a last resort. It panics me to think about that," she said, and her voice wobbled.

"I'm sure." Dario glanced away.

Delaney turned down a hallway. Dario followed but stopped her forward momentum by wrapping his hand around her upper arm. "For what it's worth, Delaney, I'm damned sorry you've had to go through so many tough things alone. There's no going back, but that doesn't keep me from feeling bad about the snags in our lives."

Tears welled in Delaney's eyes. Tears she didn't want Dario to see. He was almost easier to deal with when he acted hostile than this return to the sweet man she'd loved. "His room is just ahead," she said, slipping loose from Dario's light grip. "You need to wear one of these disposable masks for the time being." Taking one and putting it on, she discreetly blotted her tears away before breezing into her son's room.

"Sorry I was gone so long, Nick," she said, bending to ruffle his hair. "I see you had orange Popsicle for your snack." She touched the orange corners of his mouth.

"It was good," he said, leaning forward as she plumped his pillows. "Who's that?" he asked, pointing to Dario, who hadn't moved through the door. "Are you a doctor?"

Shaking his head, Dario stepped inside. "I'm...uh... an old friend of your mother's." He came to the foot of the bed and gave Delaney a harsh glance.

"Oh." Nick hesitated a moment, then ventured a small smile. "Do you like barns and animals like horses and cows?" He fumbled to hold up Zoey Bannerman's gift.

"Careful, don't fall out of bed." Dario leaped forward to catch the toy that slipped through Nick's hands.

"It's a farm-in-a-bag," Delaney supplied, helping Nick sit upright against the pillows. "A friend's daughter gave it to him," she added, moving his tray table from where the aide who had brought his snack must have rolled it out of the way. "Dario brought you a toy, as well," she added, wondering why Dario suddenly stood as stiff as a post. What was going on inside his head?

Reacting to Delaney's remark, the man set his box on the tray table.

Delaney could tell that Dario was having trouble gathering himself. Still, she was thrown off guard when he suddenly blurted, "My God, Nickolas could be Lorenzo at the same age. His eyes, nose, hair and the shape of his face are total Sanchez."

Delaney clutched at Nick's pajama top. "He has

my paler skin and my freckles," she declared, touching Nick's nose. She had to look away from the pain she saw in Dario's dark eyes as the truth hit him—he was a father. Nickolas was his son. She felt guilty and defensive at the same time as she watched him reach blindly for a bedside chair and drop into it as if his knees buckled.

"Are you sick?" Nickolas asked, eying the stranger.

"Shh, Nick." Delaney hurriedly unzipped the barn to let the plastic animals fall with a clatter on the metal table. "Dario came to see you after a long plane ride. He's probably jet-lagged."

"Did he come from farther away than Lubbock? I didn't like riding in the plane. It made my stomach jiggily."

His movements rigid, Dario opened the box and set the fire truck next to the barn. There were firefighters, ladders and even a Dalmatian fire dog.

"Delaney, take a break." It sounded like an order and Dario's voice was brittle. "I'm doing my best not to say exactly what's on my mind, but at the moment I'm finding it hard to be in the same room with you."

Stung, she knew deep down, though, she deserved some of that anger. She *had* cut the man out of Nick's life. He probably did need time, but their issues had to be handled away from Nickolas.

Delaney was on the verge of saying as much when Nick grabbed her hand and declared, "Mommy, make the bad man go away. I don't want your old fire truck!" His dark eyebrows drew together as he pushed Dario's gift off the tray table.

Caught in the middle between the two people who both had claims on her heart, Delaney watched Dario crumble beneath Nick's defense of her. She felt Dario's hurt, and gently chastened her son. "Nick, that's no way to treat a guest, especially when he brought you a really nice gift."

"It's okay." Dario got up. "He's right, Delaney. And you were right, too. I did have a long flight. I'll go back to my hotel, and come visit another day. Please, keep the truck, Nickolas. My brothers and I loved fire trucks when we were all your age. This one, the ladders roll up and down. It'll be a good addition for your farm." Picking it up, Dario again set it and the other pieces on the table.

"You have brothers?" Nick's bluster fled as quickly as it'd come.

"Two." Dario held up two fingers. "One is older and one younger than me. And we have a much younger sister. She's back at the hotel, but I know she'd like to visit you."

"I wish I had brothers," Nick said. "Or a sister, I guess. Or a dog of my own," he said, picking up the Dalmatian.

Delaney straightened his sheet. "When you get well, little cowboy, I already promised you we'd go to the animal shelter and pick out a dog."

Dario, cut out of their conversation, edged toward the door. Before he reached it, a tall man wearing glasses and a rumpled white lab coat strode briskly in. "Oh, hello," he said, glancing from the chart he clutched to the man he'd almost bowled over. "I'm Dr. Von Claus." He extended his free hand to Dario, but his gaze darted to Delaney, then to Nickolas.

"I'm Dario Sanchez. Are you the doctor Delaney

said would arrange for me to take something called an HLA-matching test?" Dario dropped the doctor's hand.

"I am. Per Dr. Blair's request I left a standing order downstairs at our lab. It's on lower level one," he added.

Dario's head came up sharply. "Dr. Blair?" He blinked a couple of times.

"Delaney," Dr. Von Claus explained. "I assumed you knew she's a veterinarian."

"Oh, of course. Sorry, I had other things on my mind."

"No doubt," the doctor said smoothly. "I also left orders for DNA testing. Our lab techs can do both tests with one blood draw. We may as well arrange for a health exam, too. Get that out of the way, should you be the marrow match we're all hoping for. You may wish to return home afterward as it can take three weeks or more for the results."

"That long?" Dario turned to Delaney for confirmation. "Is that for the DNA? If so, there's no need to run it." Dario's gaze shifted to Nickolas.

She and the doctor saw Dario's face soften.

"Ah," Dr. Von Claus said. "I see you recognize the similarities between yourself and my patient."

"Dario?" Delaney breathed out his name in a single question as she moved toward him.

"It's so obvious," he mumbled.

"Be that as it may," Dr. Von Claus said, "HLA tests can take three weeks or longer. I'll request a rush, but I must caution you both to prepare for disappointment. Physical similarities have no bearing on the markers required to make a good marrow donor."

"I do understand since I'm not a match," Delaney said. "Next weekend I have two friends coming from

La Mesa to help me conduct another cold donor drive in a predominately Latino neighborhood." She aimed an apologetic shrug at Dario.

"Good, good," said the doctor. "Delaney, will you direct Mr. Sanchez to the lab while I have a look at Nick? Oh, nice fire truck," the doctor noted as he set down his chart and pulled out his stethoscope.

Delaney trailed Dario to the door. "You're sure about canceling the DNA?" she murmured, meeting his eyes after they stepped out of the room and removed their masks.

"Nickolas is *all* Sanchez," Dario declared as he flung his mask into the trash receptacle.

"Half," Delaney stressed, her knees weak with trepidation. Dario had thrown her a curve ball and now sounded too possessive.

"If the result of the blood test is so crucial to his recovery, why does it take so long?" Dario demanded.

"I'm sorry I didn't mention the length of time. I imagine you'll want to wait for the results at home."

"You imagine wrong, Delaney. I'm not leaving. I fully intend to get to know my son. So, make sure I can come and go at will during visiting hours."

He hopped into an open elevator, but Delaney remained in place, her throat tightening in fear even as the elevator door snicked shut. Get to know *his* son? Panic beat war drums in her head. She didn't know any family lawyers. But she needed to find one fast. And how much would it cost? She pictured her dwindling bank account.

Chapter Five

Still glued in place, Delaney got a huge surprise when the elevator again opened, and Dario exited and crossed to her looking sheepish. "I…uh…don't know where the lab is."

Before she had to answer, Delaney was relieved to see Dr. Von Claus exit Nick's room.

"Oh, good," he said, "I'm glad I caught you both. I got the green light to move Nickolas into a three-bed ward with other children in the study." He gave them the room number in an adjacent wing on the same floor. "Mr. Sanchez, I'm heading to the lab now, if you'd like to follow me."

"Yes. But first, I have a question about something Delaney said. Why is there a need to hold another recruitment? What if I am a match?"

"As a rule, immediate family members can have strong markers, which is why we prefer to test them first. However, parents aren't a sure match when it comes to marrow or peripheral blood stem cells. That's the whole reason for donor banks. Strangers can sometimes be the only match."

"It sounds like a crapshoot," Dario said, his face

showing his surprise. "I have brothers. Should they be tested?"

"And a sister," Delaney said.

"Not her." Dario scowled. "We have different mothers."

"Yes, your siblings should be tested. I also recommend testing your parents. Blood markers can skip generations."

"My mother died a long time ago. My father has health issues. But I will contact my brothers now if you can arrange for their tests to be done in Buenos Aires."

"Certainly," Dr. Von Claus said, and Dario took out his cell. Phone to his ear, he paced in front of Nick's closed door.

Delaney knew he'd connected with Vicente from the way Dario's voice spiked in anger. Although they spoke mostly in Spanish, she understood they were arguing. Soon it was obvious the phone had been passed to his father. His tone changed, became more respectful, but from his half of the conversation, it was evident the elder Sanchez wanted Dario to return home at once.

The doctor checked his watch and frowned.

Touching his arm, Delaney said, "You go on. I'll see Dario finds his way to the lab when he finishes his call."

"You have my cell number. Have him leave me a message with a hospital name where they'll want tests done, if they agree. It's a shame something so crucial can cause deep rifts within a family." Shaking his head, the doctor left. Dario continued pacing, and his voice got firmer the longer he talked. Delaney winced. At last he ended the call and put the phone back in his pocket, then rubbed the back of his neck. Only then did he glance around. "Where's the doctor?" He seemed surprised to find he and Delaney were alone.

"He had to go," she said. "I'll walk with you to the lab."

Nodding, Dario darted down the hall to the bank of elevators.

She caught up and relayed the doctor's instructions. "That's assuming you got anyone to agree to be tested."

"Lorenzo will. He'll check with our two cousins who work on the *estancia*. Papa refused. And Vicente is angry that I didn't go through with DNA."

"What did you tell him? My Spanish is sketchy."

"That the boy is more Sanchez than Blair. Surely you see that." Dario hit the elevator button four times in succession.

"Again let me remind you, 'the boy' has a name," she snapped as the elevator opened, and they entered an empty car. She wasn't going to admit to anything until after she talked to a lawyer about custody.

Dario merely arched an eyebrow at her.

Once the elevator reached the basement, Delaney held it open and pointed down the hall to a glass door on which *Lab* was stenciled in large black letters. "Just go in and give the clerk your name. Tell them Dr. Von Claus ordered HLA testing for you."

Dario caught her eye, as he stepped out. "When will I see you again?"

"I'm not sure. I...need to find a place to rent so I can get out of my room at the motel. And I have a lot to do to coordinate the area recruitment. You heard Dr. Von

Claus say where they were moving Nick. I'll add you to his authorized visitor list on my way upstairs now."

"Okay, but we need to arrange time for a serious talk."

Her stomach dove. Part of her wanted to ask him what he wanted to talk about. Another part of her was afraid of the Pandora's box any such talk might open. Something had changed for Dario once he saw Nick. Nothing had changed for her. Nickolas was her son.

"I'm holding the elevator. I should go." She stepped back and released the door, but felt a stab of remorse. It was wrong for her to avoid him, but she needed to know where she stood legally.

She took a walk around the grounds outside to clear her head, cursing every sloppy emotion that had over-come her when she first held their baby—emotions that had prompted her to list Dario as Nick's father on his birth certificate.

Once back on Nick's floor, she set aside her wor-ries and donned a mask.

Nickolas held his beloved stuffed cow and his new fire truck. "Mommy, where have you been? One nurse said somebody's going to move me. I was afraid you wouldn't be able to find where I went," he said fret-fully.

Someone had started an IV for him. She hugged him and touched his hot forehead. "Oh, honey, I'll al-ways know how to find you. And it'll be nice to share a room again with other kids." As was her habit, she feathered her fingers through his hair, and as had be-come his habit, Nick ducked to avoid her touch.

"Will the man who gave me this fire truck know where I get moved?"

Delaney straightened and massaged her throbbing temples. "He will, Nick, and he wants to visit you again. Is that okay?"

"Uh-huh. I like the fire truck. I told him I didn't want it, but I do."

"It's okay, honey. He didn't mean to sound angry."

Nickolas yawned. "I'm sleepy."

Delaney noticed his face was flushed and his eyes were bright. She set the back of her hand on his cheek, not liking how warm he felt. "You probably need a nap, but I want to see if the nurse will take your temperature."

Nick mumbled, "'Kay, but they tooked it already." He cuddled his cow.

Stepping out of the room, Delaney flagged a nurse she knew had tended Nick before. "Nurse Trish, Nickolas feels hot to me. He's really hot, and I see someone started an IV while I was out."

"That was me. You're right, his temp is up, and he was complaining of joint pain, so I spoke to Dr. Von Claus and he ordered hydration and meds. Oh, he also canceled the order to move Nickolas to a ward until we see if his fever is infection-based."

"Nick thinks someone is on their way to move him. He's going to be disappointed. He likes having roommates. Goodness, this came on fast. The doctor just saw him."

"I know. Sometimes that happens. I'm sorry, but if he's coming down with a cold or other infection, we don't want it going through a ward of children who already have immune deficiencies."

"Of course. I'll explain it to him. Oh, and can I add

someone to his visitors' list?" Delaney asked, thinking Dario would blame her if there was an issue.

"You mean the man who visited your son earlier?" The nurse smiled. "Is he Nick's uncle? They look a lot alike."

Shaken by the bold observation, Delaney said, "Not his uncle." She sighed. "A relative who has traveled a long distance, though." Delaney left it at that. She needed to settle things, and soon. If Dario came around often, the staff who tended Nick would certainly see the resemblance. It'd only be a matter of time before someone in all innocence asked Nick about his father.

"Unless Nick has a virulent infection, I doubt Dr. Von Claus will isolate him. We'll continue to ask visitors to wear masks."

"No problem. I'll go in and tell Nick he's staying put a while longer. He said he's sleepy. While he naps I need to leave the hospital for a while, in case he wakes up and asks for me."

"Certainly." A call light down the hall blinked on. The nurse saw it and excused herself.

Delaney went back into Nick's room. He was sound asleep. She loosened his grip on the fire truck, thinking that might wake him. It didn't. She set the truck on his bedside table. Hating to leave without telling him about the altered plans, yet anxious to find legal counsel, Delaney felt as jumpy as a flea on a hot skillet. As worried as she'd been during Nick's first illness, she hadn't felt weighed down like she did now, facing possible shared parenting. Yet no matter how awkward, that was her situation.

She took out her cell phone with reluctance, crossed to the window and punched up Dario's cell number.

"It's Delaney," she said when he answered. "Nick's fever has spiked. Until it drops they won't move him. When you visit again, he'll likely still be in the same spot."

"A fever? Does that mean he's taken a turn for the worse?"

"I don't know. Dr. Von Claus put him on an IV with saline for hydration and meds. Nick is sleeping now. When I got back to the room he was hot and fussy. Look, I have some errands I need to run while he's napping. You have the doctor's number if you want to touch base and see what's going on. The nurse said Nick may have developed a cold or other infection. Masks are still required. I hope you're okay with that."

"I can follow rules, Delaney. Is this more serious than you're letting on? You sound stressed."

"Sorry, it's because I can't be in two places at once. I have things to do, but I don't like to leave Nick when he's has a downturn."

"I can come back and give you a break to go take care of your business. If you think Nickolas will accept me hanging around, that is."

Guilt heaped upon more guilt. Dario was being so nice, while she plotted ways to limit his options as Nick's father.

"I guess your silence means it's a bad idea."

"No, no, I was thinking. I'd appreciate you spelling me. He tends to catnap, so he may be awake by the time you get here. I hear talking in the background. You're not still at the lab, are you?"

"I'm at the hotel. Maria Sofia is pestering me to ask if she can see him. She bought Nickolas a box of

dinosaurs today. I'm trying to tell her if he isn't feeling well she should wait until he's better."

"One of you can read to him if he gets too excited.
I have some of his favorite books in the nightstand
drawer."

"All right, we'll see you in fifteen minutes or so."

Delaney used the time to add both Dario and Maria
Sofia to Nick's approved list of visitors. The list had
grown in one day to include Jill and her family, and
now Dario and his sister. But none of his doctors had
said to limit his number of visitors.

Then she called the bone marrow transplant office.
In the process of setting a time and date for the recruitment drive, she mentioned needing to find a family
lawyer near the hospital.

"Have you been in touch with family services at the
hospital?" the cheery BMT coordinator asked Delaney.

"I didn't realize they had such a service. I've recently brought my son here from Lubbock. I'm still
learning my way around this larger facility," she admitted.

"Check at the information resource center in the
lobby. If their legal advisor can't answer your questions, Dr. Blair, I know she will put you in contact
with someone in the community who can help. And
they're mindful of the financial needs of cancer patients' families."

"Thank you. That is another concern. I'm grateful you have volunteers who will post my flyers. My
friend said she'd overnight them to me. I'll get them
to you tomorrow."

"That's good. Time is always of the essence in any

of our donor drives. Often people don't realize how badly donors are needed."

"So I've learned."

"We've had fair luck gathering donors here. San Antonio has a deeply rooted Latino population."

"I hope someone out there has the blood markers Nickolas needs. Again I thank you for your help, and I'll see you tomorrow." Delaney ended the call feeling more hopeful than she had since Dario agreed to be tested. She crossed her fingers that someone would be a perfect match for Nick.

Nick's door opened quietly and Dario appeared, looking apprehensive. Because he probably couldn't see her by the window, Delaney rushed over to greet him.

Looking relieved, he stepped fully inside, and Maria Sofia tiptoed in behind him. She dropped a gift bag in a chair and flung her arms around Delaney. Delaney froze, then relaxed and returned the girl's hug. They all turned toward Nick's bed, where he slept with both arms around his stuffed cow.

"Oh, he's adorable," Dario's sister exclaimed softly through her mask. Her eyes twinkled as she moved the gift bag, which Delaney assumed held the toy dinosaurs, and sat in the chair.

"I told you he's Lorenzo at the same age," Dario murmured, his gaze never wavering from the sleeping boy.

Didn't she want everyone to adore Nickolas? Biting the inside of her cheek, she continued to feel anxious. Dario broke the spell when he leaned close to her ear and whispered, "Has his fever gone down? He's not sleeping fitfully."

Delaney went to Nick's bed and lightly set a hand on his forehead. "I believe he is cooler. Sometimes the meds they add to his IV lower his temperature quickly."

Dario frowned. "The IV is new since I was here. Sorry I didn't notice. His arm is so little. *Merced.*"

"It pains me to say he's really good about shots, IVs and other tests. He's had way too many done in his young life. Should you be the ideal donor, Dario, an IV stick is nothing compared to the process of donating or receiving marrow. Did you read the brochures I left with Maria Sofia at your ranch?"

Dario closed his eyes and nodded briefly.

Maria Sofia curled her hand around his rigid lower arm. "All will be well," she said with the surety of the young and carefree.

Delaney first stiffened, but then drew a modicum of strength from the girl's conviction. "Uh, listen, I should run out and take care of my errand," she muttered, deliberately patting her watch. "The chairs here are quite comfortable. He may sleep until I get back. But if he wakes, tell him I'll be back soon. Give him a minute to get acquainted. I promise, Maria Sofia, the dinosaurs will be a huge hit."

She opened one of the bedside drawers and took out her purse, then set a couple of children's books next to the lamp. "Nick never gets tired of having someone read his favorite Dr. Seuss books."

Dario kept pace with her to the door. "Don't feel you need to kill yourself rushing to get straight back here. I want to apologize for acting like the backside of a donkey earlier. A hundred reactions bombarded me. I thought I was prepared, but I wasn't. At first all I could do was blame you for..."

Delaney saw his jaw tense, and his Adam's apple slide up and down as he swallowed several times. Compassion for him welled up in her, in spite of her legal questions. Tucking her chin to her chest, she slipped out of the room. "I have to go," she said, tearing off her mask as she shut the door. Afraid of what else he might say to her, she dashed for the stairs and clattered down the four levels. She was out of breath at the bottom, and had to stop for a cup of free coffee in the waiting room to steady her nerves before she went in search of the family services department.

Making her way to the patient support desk, Delaney signed in with her name and Nick's name and patient number, and noted her desire to speak with a family counselor or legal adviser. She took a seat in an almost empty waiting area until the receptionist, who had been on the phone while she'd filled out her registration form, beckoned Delaney up to the counter.

"You're in luck, Dr. Blair. Two people canceled their appointments with Betty Holcomb, our patient legal adviser. If you'd fill out this three-page information document, I'll slot you into one of the cancellations."

Delaney took the clipboard and pen. "Thank you. Can you tell me the fee for the first visit?"

"Our attorneys work pro bono, Dr. Blair. Should you need representation in court, those fees are set on a sliding scale."

"That's good to know. I just have some legal questions. I hope I don't need to go to court." Hugging the clipboard, Delaney had second thoughts as to whether she should be here taking up the busy lawyer's time.

The receptionist offered a warm smile. "If you answer the questions as fully as you're able, I'm sure Ms. Holcomb will be able to point you in the right direction."

Realizing she hadn't budged, Delaney scooted back to her seat to begin laying her life bare on the form. The questions about the reason for her visit delved deeply into her past. And because her relationship or lack thereof with Dario sat at the crux of her coming here, she was forced to put down that her father had allegedly run Dario off the ranch and threatened to harm his family business.

She felt totally wrung out by the time she reached the end of the third page. But she'd tried to set out her concerns about Dario being in her son's life.

"Ms. Holcomb is ready to see you."

"Uh, sure." Delaney had been staring at her answers to these personal questions, and she sprang out of her chair now.

The attorney looked like the least intimidating person Delaney had ever met. Short, plump and middle-aged, the lawyer wore black-rimmed glasses and had shoulder-length graying hair. Her pant suit showed signs of wear, and her blouse had a coffee stain she didn't seem to care about.

"Dr. Blair," she said, smiling as she took the file from the receptionist with her left hand while extending her right to Delaney.

"I'm a veterinarian," Delaney said. "I always feel a need to make that distinction when I'm in a hospital filled with medical personnel."

"Titles are overdone, in my opinion. I'll use Delaney if that's all right. And, please, make it Betty. Jennifer," she said to the retreating receptionist, "when you have time would you call downstairs for some coffee?" She led Delaney to a flowered settee beside a short-legged, glass-topped table that could have been the centerpiece in someone's family room. At once Delaney felt the knot in her belly unfurl.

"Give me a moment to read your file. My, you have beautiful handwriting for a doctor," Betty said, glancing up with a grin.

Delaney felt herself blush. "I log my patient records in on a computer," she confided.

Betty scanned each page. A young man arrived with coffee about the time she set the file on the table and pulled a small blue notebook out of one of her jacket's patch pockets.

"Jarrett, thanks so much for indulging my need for an afternoon pick-me-up." In an aside to Delaney, the woman said, "Please, help yourself to cream or sugar. Jarrett, I trust your grandparents got the notice of reduction in their house payment?"

Jarrett beamed. "Yes, Betty. Grandma thinks you're an angel."

The lawyer laughed heartily. "Glad I could help. You and your brother just continue making time for your studies."

"Count on it," he said, grinning from ear to ear as he took his gangly body out of the room and closed the door softly behind him.

"Nice boys," she said to Delaney. "Both dropped out of medical school to take jobs in order to pay outrageous costs a shyster banker charged their grandmother when he refinanced her home. Now, let's get down to the brass tacks in your life." Leaning forward, the lawyer doused her coffee with cream and sugar. "I have to admit, out in the community where I work with single moms, the biggest complaint I hear is from women who want their exes to take responsibility for their offspring. Did I read your concerns correctly? You hope your ex fades back into the woodwork?"

Frowning, Delaney set her mug on the table and placed her hands in her lap. "If I implied Dario is my ex, I'm sorry." She rubbed the back of her neck. "It's embarrassing to admit my son is the result of a one-night stand. It's the truth, I guess, even though we spent weeks talking, laughing, riding together and boating. In all that time it's the only night we spent as lovers."

"No, I got that. I commend you for buckling down and making your son a home. You noted this is Nickolas's second bout with leukemia. Tough break for him and you. Could you clarify why you didn't contact his father during his first illness, or before that?"

"It was a matter of pride. Though our time together was brief, we were inseparable for the few weeks Dario was in town. I thought we both fell in love. The day after we slept together, he vanished. I felt like a fool. I only contacted him because Nick's need for a marrow donor is desperate. His doctors convinced me to travel to Argentina to see Dario. Our meeting wasn't pretty." Delaney picked at a loose cuticle. "He accused me of lying, and his older brother was abominable. Dario claims my dad threw him off our ranch and also caused them business problems. I only have his word on that. He insisted on a DNA test, as if I'd lie. But when he got here, the minute he saw how much Nick resembles his side of the family, he dropped that request, and his whole attitude…changed. I need to know where I stand if he…wants more than visitation."

"So, in a nutshell, you're concerned he'll demand equal custody?"

"In truth I put off thinking that sometime in the future Nick would ask about his dad. Dario never attempted to get in touch. I certainly didn't suspect that my father drove him away. You see, my dad died suddenly, before I learned I was pregnant. My life changed drastically. Dario's defection was only one hurt among many." In a few words she explained what it had been like on her end. "Dario's had his own troubles. There was a car wreck that maimed his dad and killed his stepmother. Nevertheless, I don't get the feeling Dario would have ever tried to contact me."

Betty took another drink from her mug. "Do you mind me asking why you put the young man's name on your son's birth certificate if you hadn't heard from him in at least nine months?"

Huffing out a breath, Delaney reached for her coffee. "At the time I felt so alone. My dad's lawyer urged me to put my baby up for adoption. When I think back, I know Nick's birth was so emotional. I had this baby who stared up at me with serious eyes—his father's soul-searching, coal-dark eyes. I don't know what possessed me, but it seemed wrong to write 'unknown' for his father. So I listed Dario. I made Nick's middle name Sanchez and Blair as his last name."

"Well, a family court judge wouldn't care what possessed you. Unless you can prove he's unfit to co-parent, all of the family court judges I know would applaud if Mr. Sanchez asks for some parental rights. Are you sure that's what he'll do?"

An icy knot formed in Delaney's stomach. "No, but he's asked to talk, and I've been avoiding a discussion. I wanted to understand my rights for after Nick recovers. Even with a marrow transplant, he'll need medical follow-up. Do you think a judge would, say, order me to send Nick to live in Buenos Aires half of every year?"

"Not until doctors pronounce him well."

"That could be within a year of him receiving marrow. His doctors say kids Nick's age recover fast. So he could be five or six and be forced to go live part-time with virtual strangers?"

"I don't want to lie to you. It's possible. Many families make that adjustment."

"But...Dario's father and older brother are autocratic. What if they decide Dario should have Nickolas full-time? Would an Argentinian court grant him total custody? I've read of that happening in other countries." She felt her hands shake.

"I don't know." Betty scribbled in her notebook. "I'd be happy to make some inquiries. I can see you're worried. Try to keep an open mind. Don't waste precious energy on outcomes that are down the road. Get your son well first."

Delaney rubbed her damp palms on her thighs. "Yes. One other question. Nickolas doesn't know Dario is his father. I assumed he'd fly in, take the tests and fly out again. But now he's staying at least until the HLA results are back. That could take weeks."

"You need to tell him."

Delaney glanced away. "I do. They look alike. One nurse on his floor asked if Dario was Nick's uncle."

"All the more reason to be up front. Even little children have a sixth sense when it comes to things adults try to hide."

"What if Nick gets really attached to Dario during his time here? I can imagine him sobbing his heart out after Dario goes home."

"Nickolas, or you?"

Delaney gave a start.

The lawyer stood and gathered her notebook and Delaney's file. "I see I took you by surprise. Sorry to be so blunt, but I've been in family counseling a long time. I'll look into your concerns about Argentine courts, and touch base when I get answers. Meanwhile I'll advise you as I do all clients in issues of child custody. Cases of abuse are irreconcilable. You, on the other hand, may have common ground on which to consider reconciliation. If that fails, you need to work together on what is best for your child."

"We've let too much time pass for us. But I promise I'll think about what you've said. Thank you for fitting me into your schedule. Some wise person said forewarned is forearmed."

Chapter Six

The ache in her chest was back. Sometimes it seemed perpetual to Delaney. It had disappeared after Nick went into remission. Those had been their best, most carefree eighteen months. He had been happy and energetic—normal. Her vet practice had thrived. Now their lives were on hold again, and with an added threat that, once Nick got well, she might have to send him off for part of each year to be raised by Dario.

It was one of the depressing thoughts plaguing her as she trudged upstairs. Betty hadn't sugarcoated reality. Until his death, her dad had shielded her from problems. She'd been younger than Nickolas when her mother got caught out on the ranch in a torrential rainstorm culminating in a flash flood in which she drowned. From then on her dad had served as both parents. He'd been an ideal father, which was why she'd been so flummoxed to learn his finances were in shambles. But she had dug in and had faced each obstacle head-on. It hadn't been easy, but that method had served her well then. It would now, she decided, exiting the stairwell on Nickolas's floor.

The door to his room stood open. Delaney heard voices and Nick's giggle. He hadn't had much to laugh about of late. What mother wouldn't lay all her worldly possessions at the feet of anyone who could make her sick child happy? Even if that person was the bane of her existence.

She paused before going in. Nick sat up in his bed. Dario was sitting close by on his left, while Maria Sofia's chair was on the right.

Delaney noticed the white cotton bedspread had been bunched into peaks and valleys—a veritable Jurassic Park for Nick's new plastic dinosaurs. They'd used the fencing and trees from Nick's farm-in-a-bag.

Even as Delaney hesitated to go in and interrupt, Dario began to read from the book he held. His deep, slightly accented voice touched her in a way that she hadn't been touched in a long time. Whatever he said about a T. rex was accompanied by growling sounds from Maria Sofia as she wiggled her fingers under the covers. That caused Nick to clap his hands, but then he grabbed his triceratops and moved him away from the T. rex. At the same time, he glanced up.

"Mommy, Mommy," he sang out, "come see what Tía brought me."

Aunt? The blossoming smile froze on Delaney's lips.

Dario bounded out of his chair and rushed to her side. "Step with me into the hall," he said urgently. "I can explain."

Because all she could do was blink, Delaney didn't resist him hustling her outside. "I neglected to tell Maria Sofia of our arrangement, Delaney. She didn't know we'd agreed to tell Nickolas I was an old friend of yours. When he woke up, I introduced her as my sister, Maria Sofia. He had trouble wrapping his tongue around her name. She blurted out to call her Tía Maria, or Auntie Maria. On his own he shortened it to Tía. I yanked her off into a corner and forbade her to so much as hint at my real relationship to him. I don't know what else to say, he latched on to using Tía."

She stood rubbing a chill from her arms. "He's led a sheltered life. I'm not sure he knows what an aunt is."

"Dayo," Nick shouted. "Bring Mommy back. I want her to see my dinosaurs."

Wincing, Dario tugged on his earlobe. "Maria Sofia and all our family call me Dayo. Nick picked that up right away." He gestured with the dinosaur book that he still held open. "I know you didn't expect my visit to get so complicated. I'm sorry."

She believed him. Delaney came to the conclusion she'd wrestled with since her conversation with Betty Holcomb. "We can ameliorate that by telling Nick the truth."

Dario looked stunned. "Do you mean that?"

"Yes." Delaney threaded her fingers through her hair and let the strands fall around her face. "Initially I expected you to have the test done in Buenos Aires. I never thought ahead to what we'd say if you were a marrow match and had to come to Texas. At our first meeting you acted like such a jerk, I figured you'd have your blood work and leave again. You threw me for a loop when you asked to meet Nick. Telling him you were an old friend seemed innocuous. The last thing I wanted was that he'd get attached to you and be hurt when you went back to Argentina."

Dario made a choking sound, but Delaney continued speaking. "You decided to stay, and you have a

right to spend time with him. So tell him the truth. I'll
deal with the fallout after you go back home."

"That was a mouthful. I think I followed you. I was
a jerk, Delaney, and I'm sorry. I don't deserve the gift
you just gave me. But I'll accept it." He made a fist
out of his free hand and tapped it over his heart, then
stretched his arm toward her, opening his hand.

"Stop," she said, stepping out of his reach as she
felt heat surge to her cheeks. She remembered that
gesture. He'd done the same at her bedroom door the
morning he had disappeared from her life. That fact
apparently didn't register with him. He probably meant
it as a thank-you, but she remembered it as a substi-
tute for "I love you."

"Mommy! Dayo!" This time Nick's voice warbled,
and Maria Sofia appeared at the door.

"What's up, you two? Delaney, is everything okay?"

Dario answered. "She just gave me permission to
tell Nickolas I'm his father. Now I don't know how to
go about doing that."

He did look flustered, and Delaney found that en-
dearing. "Let's go so I can check out his dinosaurs.
I'm sure you'll find a way that feels right. You don't
have to march in there and do it now, Dario."

"Right." He blew out a pent-up breath and headed
back into the room.

Maria Sofia hung back and hugged Delaney again.
"Thanks."

Delaney pulled back in surprise. "For what?"

"For not throwing us both off Nick's visitor list because I screwed up."

Delaney laughed. "I'd already planned to give Dario
the green light. Lies get messy, and someone made me

see this had the potential to be a disaster. I'm not a saint, Maria Sofia. I'm still not sure it's a good idea. It's just…my heart is so divided."

The girl tucked an arm through Delaney's. "You're human. A nice human. I've so longed for a sister. I'm Nick's aunty. Doesn't that make us sisters?"

Delaney reeled to a halt. "Not really, Maria Sofia. Dario and I have a child by accident, not design. But we can be friends," she assured quickly, because the girl suddenly looked downcast.

Dario had already retaken his seat and had gone on reading the story.

"There you are, Mommy." Nick bounced a little and stretched out a hand. "Come, see my dinosaurs. I've got two of each kind."

Taking his hand, Delaney bent and kissed his forehead. "Cool. Your dinosaurs and you," she said around a smile. "I think the medicine Dr. Von Claus ordered lowered your temperature. Yay."

"I feel okay." He yanked on his mother's arm, so she again bent to his level. "They talk funny," he whispered loudly, pointing to his visitors. "But I like them, Tía and Dayo," he clarified. "Can they come see me again?" The last was said as he peeked around his mom and gazed at Maria Sofia and Dario.

Delaney grinned and tapped her son's nose. "They probably think we talk funny, Nick."

From the way his lips pressed together and his forehead knotted, it was plain he was giving this some serious thought. "Can we be fambly?"

"Uh…" Gulping, Delaney's head swiveled between Maria Sofia, who had taken the chair nearest to her, and Dario, who suddenly bolted upright, wildly but silently imploring Delaney to help.

Maria Sofia grasped Nick's wiggling foot. "That's a bloody marvelous idea."

Dario scowled at his sister. "You're not in England now."

His sister made a face at him and shrugged.

Sinking slowly down, taking care to not sit on any dinosaurs, Delaney slid her arm around Nick and hugged him. "Nick, my little cowboy, do you remember when your friend Henry in Lubbock told you everyone had a daddy?"

The boy's eyes widened and he nodded.

Clearing her throat but looking into her son's eyes, eyes so like those of the man sitting ramrod straight nearby, Delaney plunged ahead. This needed to be said. "Well, Dario...ah...Day...o," she stuttered, "is your daddy."

For a very long moment, it seemed the room fell into such silence only Nick breathed. Finally picking up the triceratops, he said, "Henry's daddy read us a story. 'Bout a magic school bus. I like the dinosaur story better. Read more, please, Dayo. Daddy Dayo," Nick added with a shy smile.

Delaney stood up, turned aside and swabbed at a trickle of tears.

Maria Sofia saw, and she reached out and squeezed Delaney's free hand. "It's okay."

She didn't feel okay, but Delaney knew it was a secret that needed exposing. It was gratifying to hear the tremor in Dario's voice as he went back to reading aloud.

The door opened, and a nurse came in with the food

cart. She checked her watch and was surprised to see how late it was.

"Nick, honey, it's suppertime. Time to pick up your dinosaurs. I'll help."

Jumping to her feet, Maria Sofia rooted around the foot of the bed and brought out a red net bag. "They go in here."

The nurse checked Nick's temperature. "Good job. Your temp is way down. I see the IV is near enough empty to unhook it." She did that with efficiency. "His pulse is a little high, probably from the excitement of having so much company. Maybe he'd settle down and eat better if you all went to the cafeteria. But you can come back after supper until bedtime."

"Dayo's my daddy. Can he stay while I eat?" Nick's request clearly surprised the evening nurse who'd been on this shift since Nick transferred in from Lubbock. Her composure didn't crack, but she did leaf through the papers on the clipboard where she had been charting Nick's vitals.

Delaney dumped the last of the dinosaurs into the sack Maria Sofia held. "I listed them as friends. I suppose I should change that to family," she said, wearing a fretful frown of her own.

Acting nonchalant, as if adding a parent where none had existed before happened every day, the nurse nodded and finished her chores.

Delaney straightened Nick's blanket. "Honey, Dario's been here part of the morning and almost all afternoon. He probably wants to grab a bite to eat."

"I'll share," Nick said, turning pleading eyes to his mother.

"Sorry, that's not allowed, darlin'," the nurse informed him. "Your doctor relies on us knowing that you, the patient, eats what goes missing from your food tray."

Surging to his feet, Dario set the book on Nick's bedside stand. "I'm good with sticking around through his meal, Delaney, if it's okay with you."

All eyes in the room were trained on her. "If that meets protocol," she mumbled, her demeanor showing her unspoken objection. Really, every fiber in her body wanted to drag Dario out of the room. Delaney forced her mind off what felt like a ball of lead in her heart. "Maria Sofia and I can go out for a while," she added in a burst of magnanimity.

"Good idea. I'm starved. Dayo, ring me if you want to catch up to us." His sister took a shoulder bag from under her chair. She blew a kiss to Nick and hustled his mother to the door.

"Bye, Mommy. You can bring Daddy Dayo a hangaber."

Dario tossed her a curious look.

"Hamburger," she interpreted. "We can bring something back if you'd like."

"Sure." He dug in his pocket and extracted a money clip.

Maria Sofia waved him away. "I've got it."

Outside they tossed their masks in the trash. The women were in the elevator headed down when Maria Sofia turned to Delaney. "Do you hate Dayo for coming here to have his tests done?"

"No, of course not. Why would you think that?"

"You tried not to, but I saw you cry in there when Nickolas asked Dayo to stay and eat with him."

"It's only ever been Nick and me." The elevator

opened onto the lobby, and Delaney wove around others to get out. The less she said to Maria Sofia about Dario, the better. It would be easy to confide her unsettled concerns to someone. Having that person be the man's eighteen-year-old sister might not be wise.

Outside the hospital the evening air had cooled considerably from when Delaney had gone out for her walk. "Most places to eat around here are fast-food restaurants," Delaney said. "Any one of them probably makes a fair hamburger-to-go for Dario."

"I prefer something with choices. I'm not a fan of meat."

"Really? And your family raises bulls?"

Maria Sofia wrinkled her nose. "And beef cattle. We sell the bulls to rodeos or breeders and market beef on the hoof. Most of my friends in London stopped eating meat. I can eat it, I just prefer not to."

"Okay. I haven't been in San Antonio long. So until friends brought my vehicle from Lubbock, I've walked here from my motel. There's a chain restaurant in this block known for breakfast, but they offer a variety."

"That sounds fine. And if I get them to bring us Dayo's meal to go when we're almost ready to leave, his food won't get cold before we bring it back here."

They reached the restaurant, went in and were seated soon after. "It must be good," Maria Sofia said. "It's fairly busy."

Delaney glanced up from her menu. "Probably a lot of people who have someone in the hospital. I generally eat in the hospital cafeteria, but a lot of folks would rather get out of the building."

"You've spent a lot of time in hospitals I suppose, this being Nickolas's second round of care. Is that common for his type of cancer? I don't mean to be nosy, but I saw children of all ages in the rooms we passed. My impression from fleeting glimpses is that many of the patients seemed…at home. I mean their portion of the larger room looked like the one I shared at university. Bright bedspreads, family photographs and some of the older ones even have posters and iPads."

"Staff try to make it feel homey for kids who live too far away to travel back and forth for treatments. Some are daily, others biweekly. In Lubbock the rooms were more utilitarian. Nick spent weeks on the pediatric ward there. Here, with an entire floor dedicated to pediatric cancer patients, I guess they do more long-term care."

A waitress came by. Delaney's phone rang while Maria Sofia was explaining Dario's to-go order. "Hey, Jill. Are you home already? Sorry, it's noisy because I'm having supper in a restaurant." She placed one finger on her free ear and clasped the phone tight to the opposite one.

"Mack and I are in La Mesa," Jill said. "We overnighted your package of flyers to the main reception desk in the hospital. Something's come up, and we aren't able to help you next weekend with recruiting. None of us realized until we got home and looked at the calendar. Zoey and Brandy's regional soccer meet is on Saturday. That means Brandy's mom is out, as well. I'm so sorry. I doubt you'll want to wait a week to reschedule."

"No, we need it as soon as possible. I've already talked to the local marrow registry office. They're arranging a site and will distribute the flyers. I'm sure they can round up some volunteer helpers. Don't you worry. Have Zoey text me with game results."

"I will. And you let me know if you turn up a donor. Speaking of which, how did the meeting with your Argentinian go?"

"Uh, interesting. Involved answer. I'll email you."

"You'd better after that. My curiosity antennae are up."

"Well, Dario's sister and I are at supper."

"Gotcha." Jill had caught on that Delaney couldn't talk freely.

"I'm sorry you guys can't come on Saturday, but watching Zoey's regional meet is a top priority."

"You take care. I'll be anxious to get that email."

"Bye. And Jill, thanks for all your help with the flyers. Did you include an invoice?"

"Don't be silly. It's my pleasure to do this for you. Oh, Mack says he's anxious for you to get back to your practice. All of the ranchers are."

"No one more than me. It will mean Nick has whipped this disease."

"All right. You said goodbye once. Take care and keep in touch."

Putting her phone on the table, she scrubbed her face with both hands.

"Bad news?" Maria Sofia inquired, leaning back because the waitress had delivered their drinks.

Delaney dropped her hands. "Possibly. My friends who planned to help me take the important information from people willing to be tested for the National Bone Marrow Registry had to cancel. She's fluent in Spanish and I'm not. It's imperative to not screw up the names, addresses and such of new donors. And sometimes you literally have to talk people into becoming donors."

"I'm fluent, as is Dayo. We'll fill in."

Delaney studied her booth mate. "Of course you're fluent. You sound so British that I forgot. But you shouldn't volunteer Dario. He's certain he'll be a match. He thinks it's unnecessary to look for other donors even though the more Latinos in the registry the better for other kids needing donors."

"I'm sure he will join us, since it's potentially for Nickolas. My family is all bilingual. They taught Spanish and English in our schools. And my mother insisted I be tutored in French when I was young. It came in handy when I traveled around Europe."

Their food arrived. They'd both ended up ordering vegetarian omelets. Delaney poured hot sauce over her omelet. Maria Sofia gave her an odd look.

"No wonder you and Dayo hit it off so well. He puts salsa or hot sauce on almost everything he eats. So does Papa."

"As did my dad. He always said hot sauce cured whatever ailed a person." She paused with her fork halfway to her mouth as sadness washed over her. "I really miss him."

"What happened?"

"His appendix ruptured."

"Losing a parent is so difficult. I was home on summer break. One minute my mother was heading off to shop in the city. We all let her and Papa go without any special goodbyes. The accident happened in an instant, Papa said. It changed him. Made him bitter. He'd already lost one wife abruptly, and then he lost my mother."

"Yes," Delaney murmured. "Dario told me his mom died of a pulmonary embolism. On the phone, the other day, he mentioned your father was injured badly. Life can really be cruel. Uh, do you mind if we talk about something upbeat?"

"Of course."

"Tell me about your travels in Europe. I've spent most of my life in Texas except for a couple of trips to Calgary to certify cattle. Going to your *estancia* was a big deal for me."

"I love to see new places and meet new people. Europe is fine if you like history. What I'd rather do is travel around the United States and South America marketing our bulls."

"Really? Isn't that what Dario did for Estancia Sanchez?"

"He used to, but after Papa's accident, Dayo took over working directly with raising the bulls. Lorenzo and my cousin Marco split sales. Vicente complains that sales have dropped markedly. I know it's because neither Lorenzo nor Marco like selling."

Delaney pushed aside her plate and picked up her tea. "I get a sense there are road blocks to you taking over the marketing job."

"Only all of the Sanchez men." Making a face, Maria Sofia folded her napkin. "Papa and Vicente won't hear my ideas. I thought Dayo would support me. He said we'd talk about it sometime. I hope he doesn't forget."

The waitress came over. "Do you ladies want dessert?"

They both shook their heads. "Just the check,"

Maria Sofia said, "if the hamburger I ordered is ready to go."

"I'll see. You can pay at the counter and I'll bring the burger to you there."

The girl scooped up the check. "I'll get my half," Delaney said.

"My treat. It's nice for me to talk with another woman. On the *estancia* I'm stuck with all that testosterone. If I want female companionship, I have to follow our cook around. And she's busy."

"My job as a vet can be like that, too. But I do have Nick's babysitter and other female friends at home. Listen, since you're paying for our meals, I'll cover the tip."

"Fair enough."

They collected Dario's burger and headed back to the hospital. A young doctor tried to flirt with Maria Sofia, saying with a wink, "Your supper smells so good I may give up my rounds and follow you tonight." She blushed and crowded close to Delaney when she got out on Nick's floor.

"Hey," he pressed, holding open the door. "The least you can do is give me your phone number. Are you here often? I spend a lot of time here. We could meet somewhere for coffee."

Maria Sofia ducked her head and plowed forward.

Delaney could barely contain her mirth as they reached Nick's room. "You should see your face," she told the girl. "Don't they have brash men in England or Argentina?"

"In London I attended a religious all-girls' school. The nuns guarded our virtue like it was their own. At home I'm under the eagle eyes of the Sanchez Mafia."

"Now I know you're exaggerating. I saw you riding outside the walls of the *estancia*, and you didn't seem at a disadvantage when you intervened with Dario on my behalf."

The women helped themselves to masks and put them on.

Delaney stopped just inside Nick's room. "Oh, look." The women peered in at the sleeping pair across the room. Dario had turned his chair sideways to the left side of Nick's bed. Delaney saw Nick's favorite book spread open across Dario's chest, a story about a mouse that hitchhiked to the International Space Station on a shuttle craft. Nick couldn't hear the story enough. He loved the pictures, and he ad-libbed his own thoughts, insisting someday he'd be an astronaut.

At the moment, his head lolled to one side on his pillow while Dario's did the same on his chair back. The thing that most affected Delaney—seeing her son's small hand cradled in Dario's much larger one. It touched her, but it hurt, too. Dario was a stranger. It caused her breath to catch to see how quickly the two had bonded.

"I need a picture of this," Maria Sofia whispered. She handed Delaney the burger and dug her cell phone out of her purse. In seconds she'd snapped three photos. "I hate to wake them," she said, putting her phone away.

Delaney stood still, saying nothing, which prompted her companion to study her obliquely. "What's wrong?"

"No…noth…nothing," Delaney stammered. "Will you wake your brother? Here, give him his hamburger."

Maria Sofia glided to the bed. She slid the book out of Dario's loose grasp. It was enough to awaken him.

Dario blinked several times and straightened. His sleepy eyes passed over his sister first, then Delaney. Turning slightly, he looked at the softly snoring boy in the bed, and Dario sat forward, releasing Nick's hand.

Delaney realized she hadn't hid her feelings in this unguarded moment. It still rattled her to see Nick and Dario together.

"We brought your food," Maria Sofia murmured. "I'm not sure if you're allowed to eat in a patient's room. Maybe take it to the waiting area. I heard a nurse tell someone there's coffee there."

Dario got up, but his leg buckled and he might have fallen had Maria Sofia not grabbed his arm. "I guess these old bones took too many kicks from cantankerous bulls," he said, half hobbling over to Delaney, who held out the sack.

"You *can* eat in here," she said somewhat grudgingly. "With kids they relax visitor rules as long as you don't sit right next to his bed."

"The hospital may, but it's pretty clear you wish I'd never come," he said, hustling Delaney to a group of chairs in the opposite corner. He chose one and slid his mask down.

"That's not true," she said defensively at once. He gave her a knowing look. "Well, if I don't want my nose to grow like Pinocchio's, I should be honest. It is sort of true."

With a snort, Dario unwrapped his burger. He motioned for Delaney to join him. She perched uncomfortably on the edge of the chair farthest from him.

"Is this a private conversation?" his sister asked.

Not waiting for an answer, she plopped down in the middle chair.

Dario swallowed the bite he'd taken. "It's my fault we started off wrong," he said, and his apologetic tone garnered Delaney's attention. She'd been marveling that their chatter hadn't awakened Nickolas. "I've gotta admit I've smarted a long time from the way your father treated me. Our whole family has hard feelings from the financial blow your dad dealt our business."

"I swear I didn't know any of that," Delaney insisted. "I was in shock over our own financial collapse. The only reason I was able to survive Dad's double mortgaging everything we owned was that he did it to pay for my schooling. It allowed me to begin my vet practice. Otherwise I might have ended up a single mother on welfare."

Dario ate some French fries. Wiping his fingers on his jeans, he asked, "Would going on welfare have made you contact me sooner?"

"Doubtful. I filed you in with my father's bad debts." She shut her eyes and squeezed the bridge of her nose. "What purpose does rehashing any of this serve?"

"We need some middle ground."

"Why? No, I take that back." Delaney held up a hand. "If you're a donor match for Nick, *that* is our middle ground."

"Speaking of donors," Maria Sofia broke in, "Saturday, Delaney is doing donor recruiting. Her friends who were going to help her can't come. I volunteered us, Dayo. Because some of the prospects may only speak Spanish."

He frowned. "Isn't recruiting pointless? I'm sure I'll be a match."

"Even so," Delaney said, "the national donor bank needs more Latino donors."

"Okay, I'll help, but between now and then I want to visit Nickolas every day. Do you want to set a schedule?"

"A schedule?" Delaney gaped at him.

"Yes. I'd like to not always feel like you're about to plunge a dagger in my back."

"Sorry."

"You're not," he said dryly, wadding up the sack with the remaining fries. "I try to think how I'd feel if our roles were reversed. I can't."

"At least you're truthful. I can try to give you some space without hovering. Tomorrow morning I have to go down to the local donor bank. And I need to hunt up a leasing agent. In Lubbock I stayed in a home owned by the cancer chapter. It's easier to rest in a house than at a motel. I hope it's also less expensive. What if for the next few days I don't come to the hospital until after lunch? I'll spend afternoons with Nick. I suppose we can split evenings."

Dario tossed the bag into a wastebasket several yards away. His hooded gaze shifted back to Delaney. "That will work until my tests come back. We'll need to get more specific when it comes to dividing up longer periods," he said, his tone brooding. Getting up, he motioned to Maria Sofia. "We should go back to our hotel. I told Vicente I'd ring him tonight."

Maria Sofia made a face which Dario ignored.

The pair left, and it took a while for Delaney to relax her hands where they gripped her knees. The omelet tossed in her stomach as she forced herself to digest Dario's ominous parting words about dividing up longer periods with Nick.

Chapter Seven

Over the next few days it seemed to Delaney that Dario lost no time bridging any gap that existed between him and Nickolas. Each afternoon when she hurried to Nick's room, the pair's matching dark heads were together. Often Nick wore a contented smile that tore at her heart. Sometimes Dario sat reading him a book. Sometimes they played Go Fish, one of Nick's favorite card games. Or like today, they watched a rerun of some football game on the room's grainy TV. What troubled Delaney was that with every day that passed, her son seemed less happy to see her. Today, Nick frowned when she walked in.

"The game's not over, Mommy. Can you go away and come back later? Daddy Dayo and me are watching big kids play...who?" He turned to Dario and tugged the sleeve of the black T-shirt that outlined Dario's sculpted muscles. Even without her son's dismissal, those muscles were enough to cause turbulence in Delaney's stomach.

"A local high school," the man supplied. He failed to spring to his feet immediately as he'd done every other day. "I'm staying today. The nurse said Dr. Von Claus is coming by to see Nick at two o'clock." Dario placed a hand on Nick's forehead. "I think his fever has spiked again. Just when Nurse Trish mentioned moving Nick to a ward after the doctor's visit this afternoon."

"Move him? No one advised me." Delaney dropped her purse on a chair. "Our arrangement doesn't include you dealing with Nick's medical care, Dario," she snapped.

"Whoa! Why not?" He reared back.

"Because I am his guardian. His parent," she stressed, jamming her thumb aggressively against her breastbone.

Dario jumped to his feet then, his arms akimbo. "Then we'll have to see about changing that, won't we?"

That statement struck fear in Delaney's heart.

Nick sat forward, his eyes too bright in his pale face. "I can't hear the game," he said.

Dario and Delaney exchanged guilty looks at their son's complaint as Maria Sofia breezed into the room.

"Hey, you two. I could hear you when I got off the elevator. What has you snarling at each other now?" she asked. "I have good news." She produced a paper from her handbag. "I located a three-bedroom, three-bath house within a ten-minute walk of the hospital. It has a great kitchen, a covered patio and a beautiful, heated pool. I held it with a deposit, Dayo, until you and Delaney go see it and approve."

Delaney whirled. "Why would I need to see anything you rent?" Anger tinged her tone because Dario's earlier statement still grated.

"Maria Sofia." Dario turned on his sister. "I said we needed to talk to Delaney first."

"So, talk already." The girl shoved the paper with a picture of a house into his hand.

Delaney spared a quick glance at the sheet. She'd already seen stats on that house. It had looked gorgeous, but was too large and costly for her. The past three days she'd checked out most available rentals in the area but hadn't had any luck finding one she could afford. That also had her on edge. Although nothing compared to the worry of Nick's symptoms coming back.

Dario cleared his throat. "Delaney, last night Maria Sofia suggested we might all cut costs by getting out of our hotels."

His sister rolled her eyes. "Vicente popped his cork when he got our credit card bill." She turned to Delaney. "He wants Papa to insist I fly home. He says Dayo can rent a cheap room. I don't want to leave America. Say you'll consider the house, Delaney. I don't know where you're staying, but renting together makes sense. If we're all under one roof, it'll be easier to coordinate who sees Nickolas, when. And we wouldn't always have to eat out, which saves money. Like I said, the house is quite close to the hospital."

Dario took out a pen and did some figuring on the paper Maria Sofia had given him. "Even if I paid it all, it'd be less than what we're spending on two rooms at our hotel."

"How much would my share be?" Delaney asked. She'd gone to sit on the edge of Nick's bed and pulled him close to test his cheek for fever using the back of her hand.

Dario watched her and asked, "Does Nick feel *mas* warm to you?"

Bending, Delaney kissed Nick's forehead. "How do you feel, honey?"

"I feel bad, 'cause you were all talking. Now I don't know who won the game."

The three adults all turned their attention to the TV.

"What game?" Maria Sofia asked at the same time Delaney said, "Does it matter who won? I was asking if you feel sick, honey."

Dario held up a hand. "Listen a minute to the recap." The women fell silent. "Sorry, buddy," he eventually murmured, tousling the boy's hair. "The guys in the black-and-gold uniforms won twenty-one to fourteen."

Nickolas flopped back against his pillows. His lower lip trembled. "I wanted the blue guys to win. Mommy, my tummy hurts."

Delaney straightened his pajama top. "What did you eat for lunch?"

"Sketti. It wasn't as good as Miz Irene's."

"Irene Thompson is…was…Nick's babysitter at home in La Mesa."

"Isn't she still there?" Nick asked anxiously. "Where did she go?"

Delaney cuddled him close. "She is still in La Mesa, Nick. I only said *was* because you're here now. Don't worry. She phoned me last night to ask how you're doing. Once you get well and we go home, she'll baby-sit you and Sarah still."

Nickolas turned his head to look at Dario. "Maybe I won't gotta be babysat if he comes home with us. Daddy Dayo," Nick clarified.

That brought a rich laugh from Maria Sofia, who stood close enough to Dario to jab his ribs.

The statement drew a gasp from Delaney, after

which she aimed a scowl at Dario. "Are you filling his head with nonsense?" she demanded, though Dario actually seemed a bit rocked himself.

"I assure you the subject hasn't come up before," Dario mumbled. More might have been said, except that Dr. Von Claus blew into the room, the tails of his white lab coat flapping in the rush of wind he created. His voice boomed a general greeting as he descended on his patient, all the while warming his stethoscope by rubbing the diaphragm vigorously against his coat.

Everyone fell silent and watched as the doctor slid the scope under Nick's pajama top, listened intently, then went on to tap his joints and inspect his groin. Nick didn't cry, but he moaned "ow" several times.

He motioned to Delaney and Dario with the folder. "Will you two join me a moment in the hall?" His gaze flitted to Maria Sofia. "Perhaps Ms. Sanchez will keep Nickolas occupied for a short while."

"I have a new video game Nick will love," Maria Sofia said, pulling an electronic device from her voluminous bag.

Expecting her son to be overjoyed at the prospect, Delaney felt a shiver of concern travel through her when Nick only curled up around his favorite stuffed cow. But because Dario and Dr. Von Claus had already left the room, she squeezed Nick's toes and hurried out after them. She took care to close the door, but her worry increased when she heard Dario ask the question uppermost in her mind.

"Has Nick's fever returned, Doctor?"

"His temperature is up and I detect swelling in one of his lymph glands. I'm ordering a spinal tap to see exactly what's going on."

Delaney gave an involuntary shudder. Spinal taps were tedious, and Nick had undergone several during his first episode with the disease.

Stepping up behind Delaney, Dario curled a hand around her waist and drew her into the crook of his arm. The uncharacteristic move surprised her, but more surprising was that she accepted his support instead of moving away. She had faced so many carefully worded bouts of bad news alone, she couldn't begin to articulate the relief it gave her to lean on someone. Someone as strong and as warm against her chilled body as Dario.

"That's a surgical procedure, right?" Dario spoke to the doctor. "He seems so little," he murmured. "I'm sorry, but can you explain it to me?"

The doctor nodded. "We do the tap in surgery, yes. Up to now Nick hasn't had any recurrence of leukemia cells in his bone marrow, which is good. It's why we can maintain him on a low dose of radiation while we search for a marrow donor. If that's changed we'll have to restart chemotherapy. That's always harder on a patient, as Delaney can tell you."

"Tomorrow is our donor recruitment," Delaney said even though her lips felt stiff due to her deepening fear. "With luck maybe we'll turn up a match."

"Is there any chance you can ask the lab to speed up getting results from my test?" Dario asked. "I still say I'm the most likely donor. The tech downstairs skipped the preliminary cheek swab and went straight to drawing my blood for testing."

"I know how difficult this can be," Von Claus said. "But the steps are too crucial to be rushed. We do all that we can to keep a patient stable until we find a match. Every day someone in my department searches the US donor bank. Plus we've begun a daily check of the South American bank, since Nick's heritage makes it worth expanding the parameters."

"Of course you're doing all you can," Delaney said. "Waiting is just so hard."

The doctor agreed. "I'll go see if I can schedule that tap for sometime tonight. Will one of you be around when he comes back to his room? It may be quite late."

"I'll be here," Delaney said, her words colliding with Dario's, "Absolutely."

Dr. Von Claus walked away, and Dario tightened his hold on Delaney. She leaned into him to draw from his solidness, but was still caught off guard when he pressed a kiss to her temple. Feeling a tremor pass through him compelled her to slide her arms around his waist and hug him. "You're experiencing the difficult part of parenting, Dario. Sorry. I can tell this downturn in Nick's condition has hit you like a brick. It shakes me every time, too. Although I've gone through a lot of downs."

"And I should have been here with you," he said, brushing his lips back and forth across her hair above her ear.

Fighting against a different kind of feeling rushing through her, she ducked away, crossed her arms and massaged goose bumps from her arms. "What can I say? I honestly thought you'd written me off."

"We didn't have enough time to get to know each other. But what I can't make sense of is why you're so resentful of me now. I came here at your invitation." He looked her in the eye, then reached out and brushed one hand over her hair. "If I'm doing something wrong, or not doing something you think I should, tell me, for heaven's sake."

She moved away from his touch. "I find this sharing awkward."

"Why? I'd think it'd be easier on you."

"I got used to single parenting."

"That's not my fault," he responded, a little testily.

She hunched her shoulders. "I don't want to argue. Nickolas is taken with you." She put out a hand to open the door. "We need to go back. Maria Sofia will wonder what's keeping us so long."

He halted her with a touch. "So, are you okay with all of us renting the house?"

"I haven't taken time to consider it. I'm trying to stick to a budget."

"Me, too," he said. "I'd rather not give Vicente reason to rile Papa. Not that my brother isn't a good accountant. He is. Until the accident, Papa handled the *estancia* accounts. He was overly generous with our stepmother and Maria Sofia. When Vicente took over, he put all of us on strict budgets, causing some tense moments. He deserves credit for getting us in the black, though. But he can be, how do you say it… *tacaño*."

Delaney puckered her brow. From the way Dario rubbed his fingers and thumb together, like squeezing a dollar bill or a coin, she took a stab at what he meant. "Skinflint, maybe? Or tightwad? I'm guessing he has a tight rein on the purse strings."

Dario smiled. "*Stingy* is the English word I was looking for. But you have the right idea. He and Maria Sofia clash a lot over money. She does an end run around him and goes to Papa, who rarely refuses her.

He's hard-nosed about other things she does, but he shells out the cash."

"She strikes me as being strong-willed. Look how she found a house and made the decision to hold it."

"Good way to describe her. Renting a house isn't half of what's on her mind. Remind me to fill you in on her other ambitions when we get some time."

"All right. But as far as this house goes, I need to know how much my third of rent and food would be. At least being able to walk to and from the hospital will help me save on gas. Would you go check it out? Since Nick is probably having the spinal tap tonight I want to stay here."

"You trust me to say yes or no on your behalf?" he asked, following Delaney through Nick's door.

She grinned. "I trust you'll recognize a cockroach or a rat. Oh, and water stains on the ceiling wouldn't be good. Mostly, I need a dollar figure."

Dario went over and picked up the house flyer.

Maria Sofia unfolded from her chair and touched a finger to her lips. Nick had fallen asleep.

"I think his fever is down," Delaney said softly, gliding to the side of the bed. "When he sleeps with both hands above his head it shows he's relaxed. Nurses tell me that's something all kids do when they're not feverish or in pain."

"His fevers come and go so quickly." Dario said in a low voice.

Delaney nodded. "They do, and that's one reason it's so hard to know anything serious is wrong. When Nick wasn't quite two, my sitter and I thought he'd caught cold, or maybe the flu. Our local doctor saw him three times before he referred us to a clinic with up-to-date lab facilities. By then his cancer had a grip. Well, you guys live a long way from town, too. You probably know it's not easy to get access to top medical care."

"Access doesn't always mean success," Maria Sofia said. "Mama and Papa's accident was in Buenos Aires, and Mama died in the ambulance. And quick treatment didn't help Papa's back injury."

"Can we not dwell on the morose?" Dario took the paper with his figures to Delaney. "This would be the month-by-month amount each of us would pay toward rent and utilities. We would have to work out together splitting groceries. You'd know more about those costs."

"Are you sure these are right?" Delaney ran her finger across his numbers. "That's substantially less than the weekly rate I'm paying at the motel now. I'm paid through Sunday. But if this house is fully furnished and as nice as Maria Sofia claims, count me in."

"I'd like to be back here before Nick goes for his procedure. Maria Sofia, let's go now to look at the property. If it passes Delaney's requirement of no vermin," he teased, "we'll check out of our hotel. After tomorrow's recruitment, we can help you move, Delaney."

Once they left, Delaney claimed her usual chair at Nick's bedside. But her mind wandered back to how snug she had felt in Dario's arms. He'd delivered a kiss and a light brush of his mouth a second time. Both had given her comfort. But was it wise to drift under his spell? He'd already questioned why she was keeping him at arm's length. Maybe Dario hadn't thought ahead to legalities. She had, and she couldn't stand the notion of Nick flying to Argentina for split custody. Dario had mentioned the way his father's old-fashioned ideas ruled their household—ruled Maria Sofia's life—and it gave her shivers to imagine his expectations toward a grandson. His only grandson. She made a mental note to see what Betty Holcomb had found out about Argentine law. Would she risk losing total custody?

MARIA SOFIA CLIMBED into the passenger seat of the rental car and buckled in. "I'll direct you to the house. Or maybe you want to go check out of our hotel first."

"You're awfully confident I'll like this place," Dario said, easing out of the parking space.

"It's perfect!" She grinned. "How did you convince Delaney to go along with my plan? She wants to keep you at a distance."

"I know. You went to dinner alone with her. Did she give you any idea why I'm a pariah?"

"No. And I don't understand why. I mean, it pained her to do it, but she *did* tell Nickolas you're his dad."

"She still seems resentful that I didn't call once I left their ranch. I explained the circumstances," he said, frustrated. "I thought she knew that her dad ordered me never to contact her again. I might have defied him, but then Papa was in the accident. Still, shouldn't she have contacted me once she found out she was pregnant?"

Maria Sofia shrugged. "Turn left and go two houses. Pull into the first semicircular drive you see."

"Nice area. How did you manage to get it for such a good price?" Dario peered around at the neighborhood.

"It's a small world. It was pure luck that the owners are adjunct professors at the school I attended in London. They wanted to rent their home month to month because they aren't sure come September they'll teach in London again. Most people apparently want a year's lease. By the way, I noticed you gave Delaney a healthy discount."

"Yes, but don't tell her or Vicente. It's the least I can do. Delaney's never asked me for child support. It didn't come up even after she said I could tell Nick I'm his dad."

"I have a key," Maria Sofia said. "Dayo, may I ask you something personal?"

"Ask, but I reserve the right not to answer."

"Fair enough. Have you thought about what you'll do about Nick after he gets his marrow transplant and goes into remission?"

Dario hung back as his sister bounded up the steps and unlocked the front door. He said nothing even after they were both inside.

"I take your silence as a no. Is it no you haven't thought ahead, or no you're not talking because it's too nosy a question?"

Dario huffed out a sigh. "I lie awake at night thinking about it. It's not very noble or manly, but I avoid talking to Delaney about it. Waiting for a better time, I guess."

"Bollocks!"

"Papa would have fits if he heard you use that unladylike word."

Maria Sofia gave a cheeky grin. "It's a very British term, you know. I've heard it said in quite dignified circles. Besides, I figure it will come in quite handy when I take over bull sales for the *estancia*."

"That again. Lead on. Let's tour the house and make sure there isn't a single rat or cockroach."

After they'd checked every corner of the kitchen, and looked at the remaining rooms, they stepped out onto the patio. "The pool is nice, but I doubt we'll be here except to sleep," he said. "It all seems fine. I'm good with paying for a full month."

"I thought you would. As for the pool, we all can't spend every waking hour at the hospital, Dayo. If they finally move Nick to a ward with other kids, I'm guessing he won't want all of us hanging around."

"I wish Dr. Von Claus was able to settle him enough to move. So far he's heading in the wrong direction. Delaney has weathered these kind of setbacks before. She must be made of steel." Dario locked the back door and tramped on into the first of three bedrooms. "For sure she's one strong woman. I wish Papa, Vicente and Lorenzo could meet her. I know they'd change their minds about her."

"Maybe you two will get back together! Maybe she and Nick can join us at the *estancia.*"

He stopped in the middle of the hallway between two bedrooms. "I'll take the smaller side room. You and Delaney can have the pair overlooking the pool."

"So, this time I did get too nosy, huh?"

"Maria Sofia." Dario drawled her name in the way only an irritated older brother could. "Swear to me you won't bring up any of these questions to Delaney."

"Fine," the girl grumbled, leading the way out of the house. "But…"

She added something under her breath in Spanish that Dario didn't catch. It was just as well. Lord help him if she ever found out how he'd touched Delaney today. It'd been spontaneous and had felt right. Had felt good. Yes, it had happened during a moment of worry, but Delaney had been soft and pliant, and he wanted to remember it without being nagged by his too observant sister.

TWO NURSES WERE prepping Nick for his surgery. He was crying, and Delaney's stomach was a ball of nerves.

"I want Daddy Dayo," Nick sobbed. "Where is he, Mommy?"

"He and Maria Sofia went to see a house to rent, Nick. I'm sure he'll be here after your procedure." Nick had slept, and she'd read a magazine. Delaney had thought Dario would be back by now, and they'd been gone quite a while. But what could she expect? Dario wasn't really beholden to Nick. He didn't have to follow through on his promises. He paid lip service to being a dad, but really, he had no idea what it was like to stand helplessly by, suffering, when your child hurt. Oh, that was unfair. He hadn't had the chance.

Leaning over the bed, she smoothed matted dark hair off Nick's damp forehead. He was sobbing so hard his eyes were swollen and red, and the exertion made him sweat. "Hey, hey, buck up, my little cowboy. You had this procedure done in Lubbock. Mommy needs you to be brave," Delaney said, even as her insides shook and her legs went weak.

"We're going to move him to the gurney now," the older of the two nurses said. "You can walk alongside him. And you're welcome to stay with him until someone delivers his preop. Then you may either come back here or stay in the waiting area outside surgery."

"I'll stay closest to Nick," Delaney said. She was aware of the risks of anesthetic and any surgical procedure, and it left her in turmoil. Being able to exert herself in any manner helped keep her grounded.

The door opened, and Delaney couldn't believe her relief at seeing Dario's six-foot frame fill the opening. Had she, in the short time he'd been here, already come to rely on sharing some of the worry for Nickolas?

"Da—daddy Dayo," Nick spoke thickly through his streaming tears. "I don't want to go for a 'cedure."

Dario entered the room with halting steps. His frantic gaze took stock of the scene, then skipped to Delaney.

She remembered when she'd been new to all of this, and she felt sympathy for him. "Nick, honey, Daddy Dayo knows the procedure is important because it will help doctors find out how to make you well again. He's going to walk on the other side of you while we go with your transport team. Okay?" The query was aimed at Nickolas, but Delaney's eyes, over her mask, remained steady on Dario.

"'Kay," Nick said, this time making a huge effort to stop sniffling. "I want Tía to go with me, too."

Dario's big body had blocked Maria Sofia from Delaney's view. She made eye contact with the young woman, but she couldn't tell from Maria Sofia's expression if she wanted to be included. She decided to let her speak for herself.

The girl moved around her brother. "If it's all right that all of us go, Nick, I will be with you."

"It's okay, right, Mommy?" The boy checked with Delaney, his anxious eyes so similar to Dario's. For a moment, that connection rattled her.

One of the nurses skirted Dario where he still blocked the doorway and said, "Here our focus is to give our patients as much family support as we can. All of you may accompany Nick."

And so they did. Winding through the halls, Delaney and Dario could each hold one of Nick's hands as they all kept up with the transporters, who knew where they were going.

Only after they arrived outside of the double doors that led into the surgical suites, and after a preop shot left Nickolas groggy, did Dario mouth his thanks to Delaney.

She accepted with the barest hike of one shoulder before she leaned down, lowered her mask slightly and pressed a couple of kisses to Nick's cheek. "Hang tough," she said as two nurses emerged from the surgical area. They wore scrubs and white surgical masks. "They're ready to take Nick in," she told Dario.

He wasn't quite as smooth when he dropped a kiss on Nick's forehead through his mask. "Tía and I will wait with your mommy," he murmured, straightening slowly as Nick's gurney was whisked through doors that opened and closed with a pneumatic whish. "I'm not sure he understood me." Dario slid his hands into his back pockets.

"He was pretty far gone under from the preop shot. Dr. Avery—he's the pediatric oncologist in Lubbock who handled Nick's earlier bout—told me kids under sedation are helped by the sound of a voice they know. As a rule, lumbar punctures are done with a local anesthetic, but with kids as young as Nick they give a relaxer first."

Dario nodded silently.

"I saw a waiting area around the corner. Let's sit there in case anyone has questions for us. The doc doing the spinal tap will look there first for family when he's done." Delaney led the way and sat on the edge of one chair. Dario and Maria Sofia sat across from her. They all unhooked their masks from one ear and let them hang loose.

"Will it take long?" Dario planted his elbows on his knees and clasped his hands between them.

"The procedure lasts fifteen or twenty minutes, but the length of time he's in there depends on how many procedures are scheduled ahead of him, and how long they keep him in recovery. There's coffee and juice in the back corner if either of you would like some."

He sat up and glanced past other occupied seats. "I didn't notice that when we came in. But I also didn't see other people waiting here. How do you stay so calm, Delaney?"

"I wondered that, too," Maria Sofia chimed in. "He's not my son and I feel shaky. Maybe I will have coffee. Can I bring either of you some?" she asked.

Delaney shook her head. "I'll have a cup afterward. I'm wired enough without caffeine. You asked how I stay calm. I'm not on the inside. It is a surgical procedure, and inside I'm a wreck for worrying about the results."

"I see why you're so thin," he said. "I mean, thinner than I remember. I don't mean that to be critical," he said, stumbling through his words. "To the contrary. I'm sure this is only a small taste of all you had to go through on your own before." He cracked his knuckles. "All I can say is I think you have amazing strength, Delaney."

"He's not trying to flatter you," Maria Sofia said, rising from her chair. "He said the same thing to me at the house."

"Oh! The house. How did that go?" Delaney asked.

"He approved and we moved our stuff in already. You and I get the biggest bedrooms," Maria Sofia said, then wove her way to the coffeepot. "You can bring your things anytime you're ready."

"I almost forgot about the house," Delaney said. "No cockroaches or water stains?"

"None. It appears to have everything we'll need. It's in a nice neighborhood."

"I'm grateful for that. I hadn't thought about walking there alone late at night. Sometimes Nick can't get to sleep. I always stay until he settles down."

"Any instance when I might not already be here with you, call and I'll come meet you. I don't want you walking alone after dark. No place in a city this size is that safe."

Delaney puffed up to say she didn't need cosseting, but his ringtone blared, causing everyone in the room to jolt out of their various stupors.

"Didn't you see the sign that said to silence your phone?" Maria Sofia chided, rushing back, stirring in powdered creamer that floated atop her coffee.

Her admonishment coming too late, Dario accepted the call and growled hello, followed quickly by, "Can I talk to you later, Vicente? I'm in a hospital waiting room. Nick's having a spinal tap. What? You what? No, I can't go to Chickasha, Oklahoma, wherever the hell that is!" He paused, listening. "I don't care if you emailed me stats and photos of our bulls. I don't care if some guy may want to buy them for the rodeo. Send Lorenzo or Marco. Sales is their job."

Maria Sofia was yanking on his arm, and he trailed off, looking at her questioningly. She'd set down her coffee cup, and now that she had his attention, she madly waved her arms and indicated that she wanted to speak with him.

"I'll phone you later," he said to Vicente in Spanish. Clicking off, he glared at his sister. "What in the devil was that all about?"

"Let me go to Oklahoma to present our bulls. It's my chance to prove to Papa and Lorenzo that I can handle our sales." Her eyes shone with excitement, and she fairly bounced in her seat. "You don't need to tell Vicente," she begged. "I don't want you to lie, but just agree to his request. Vicente will think you're going, but I'll go in your place."

"It's out of the question."

"I trained for it, Dayo. I told you I took all of those online marketing classes. Please!"

"Papa would kill me if Vicente didn't first."

"Come on," she wheedled. "Your place is here with Nickolas. How long can it take for me to fly there, show photos of our stock, convince someone who is already interested to buy, and come back with a contract?"

Dario's eyes met Delaney's. She watched their byplay with interest and spoke up. "If she doesn't mind sticking around tomorrow for the recruitment, she could be back by Thursday or Friday. She can fly from here to Oklahoma City and rent a car to drive to Chickasha."

"I don't know," Dario muttered, though it was clear

that he was beginning to cave. "Is dealing with a rodeo stockman something you'd do?" he asked Delaney.

She laughed. "Stockmen are ranchers. I grew up among those types. As a veterinarian of large animals, I regularly work with ranchers and their ranch hands. They're probably the most polite guys toward women that you'd ever hope to find, Dario."

"All right," he said slowly. "I'm sticking my neck out here, kid," he added as they all watched his petite, ladylike sister pump an unladylike fist in the air.

Chapter Eight

A doctor in scrubs came out of surgery. "Mr. and Mrs. Blair?" she called from the door to the waiting area.

Dario looked up.

Delaney sat straighter. "I'm Delaney Blair, Nick's mother."

The doctor rechecked the clipboard she held. "Good to meet you. I'm Dr. Lacy Mahoney." She stepped between her and Dario where they sat opposite one another, knelt and began to speak. "Nickolas's spinal tap report is good. For now his fluid is still free of cancer cells. He's in recovery where we'll keep him a few hours. But you know the drill. I see this isn't his first tap."

Standing, Dr. Mahoney disappeared back through the double doors, and Delaney broke down in tears.

"Why are you crying?" Dario changed seats to sit beside her. He lightly rubbed a hand up and down her back. "That sounded like good news to me."

She dried her tears on her shirt tail. "I feared the worst," she admitted. "On Nick's ward in Lubbock I saw too many kids die after a relapse. The type of cancer Nick has can expect eighty percent survival initially. But the percentage falls significantly if they relapse. I thought he'd dodged a bullet the day Dr. Avery phoned to say Nick's cancer had gone into remission. I cried then, too. Happy tears, like these ones. If you're around to see him diagnosed cancer free once he gets new marrow, I'll probably resemble a waterfall."

"I will be around," Dario declared, yanking tissues from a box Maria Sofia brought over from the table beside her chair. He dabbed Delaney's cheeks. "Why can't you believe I'm not going anywhere?"

Delaney took the tissues from him, wiping her face before she tossed them in a nearby trash bin. "Why don't you guys get yourselves some supper? I'll go back to Nick's room. He'll be in recovery an hour or so, because they want to be sure he doesn't leak fluid, so you'll have at least that long."

"You didn't answer Dayo's question. I'm curious, too," Maria Sofia said on the walk through the hallways. Evening visiting hours were always busy, and this was a large ward. "I can't figure out why you went to the trouble to track Dayo down half a world away if you don't think he'll see this through."

"You've no idea how much I want to believe he's the match and will be the one to donate marrow. The truth is I'm afraid to. I assumed I'd be the perfect donor. I wasn't. I expected the National Marrow Bank would have a donor. They didn't."

"All right, I get it," Dario said. Adapting his stride to Delaney's shorter steps, he casually looped an arm around her shoulders. Maria Sofia poked her elbow in his ribs and shot him a grin, which he ignored.

The instant Delaney reached up for his hand, Dario laced their fingers together.

His sister tapped his shoulder. "Dayo, if you give me the car keys I'll run by the house and grab your laptop so we can see Vicente's email. On the way back I'll stop at that deli we spotted, and buy sandwiches. We can eat in Nick's room again, can't we?"

"I'm not very hungry, but sure. If that's what you want to do," Delaney said.

Dario groaned. "What time is it? I forgot I said I'd phone Vicente back. What if he wants to wire me a plane ticket?" He let go of Delaney and pulled out his phone.

"Tell him you'll handle it," Maria Sofia suggested.

"Like he thinks anyone is capable but him." Dario snorted. "Okay, okay," he said because both women fixed him with twin frowns.

Waiting to peel off from the others at the elevator across the hall from Nick's room, Maria Sofia hurriedly asked what kind of sandwich they wanted.

"Chicken salad. A half sandwich if they do that," Delaney said.

"Roast beef," Dario put in. He pulled out his wallet so he could give Maria Sofia cash, along with the car keys.

Grabbing the bills, she dropped the keys in her handbag and dashed for the elevator, which was being held open by a man dressed in gray slacks and a white lab coat.

Delaney recognized him as the same young doctor who'd flirted with Maria Sofia before. She chuckled, wishing she could be a fly on the wall to watch Maria Sofia discourage him again—or not.

"What's so funny?" Dario asked, stepping to one side so Delaney could pass into Nick's room before him.

"That guy on the elevator is a young surgical resident who did everything but stand on his head to get
Maria Sofia's attention last time we ran into him."

"*Grreat.* Not only am I contemplating letting her
run off alone to Oklahoma to meet some unknown
stock contractor, now you tell me a randy resident here
at the hospital has the hots for her."

"We don't know he's randy. He's kind of cute. But
what do you mean by contemplating letting her go to
Oklahoma? I thought you agreed. *She* thinks you did."

Dario opened his top shirt button and flung himself into his favorite chair. "Papa would have a stroke
if he knew."

Delaney wet her lower lip with her tongue. "Is there
real danger of that? A stroke?"

"Oh, no. I am exaggerating. The accident crushed
several of his lower vertebrae. Outside of that his
health is good for his age. He just gets worked up when
we go against his wishes. He's an old-school patriarch,
ruler of his family and all within his domain. I can picture him sending Maria Sofia to a convent rather than
let her travel around on her own selling our bulls."

"I can picture her running away from a convent,"
Delaney returned.

Dario scrubbed both hands over his face. "Yeah.
If she makes the sales in Oklahoma, maybe I can talk
Vicente into coming down on her side. It's a cinch
Lorenzo and Mario won't care. Neither of them like
sales. They do it because Papa ordered it."

"What about you? Could they take over what you
do, working directly with the bulls? Your father might
switch them out and put you in charge of sales."

He sat a moment studying her. "Are you really interested in what goes on with our business?"

"I suppose not," she snapped, because his question felt like a zinger. Not a big surprise that he didn't want to involve her in his family's affairs. But would it hurt him to pass the time talking about the business? No matter, she wouldn't make that mistake again.

"I'm going out in the hall to phone Vicente," he said, climbing to his feet.

Delaney settled in her usual chair and opened the book she'd been reading the past few days. She paged back a chapter. Worry over Nick's on-again, off-again fevers crowded out everything else, and she couldn't remember what was going on in the story. Even now she couldn't focus well, thinking instead about how Dario ran hot and cold. Earlier, and even down by surgery, he'd been attentive. What was all his touching her about? She hadn't dreamed that kiss either. Not that it had been a kiss-kiss. Still, it showed interest, didn't it? And yet a moment ago he'd been affronted because she'd dare ask a casual question about his family's livelihood.

She took the opportunity while Dario was gone to locate the legal adviser's card, and call her to ask if she'd gotten any information about Argentine law when it came to paternity. Her concerns increased after hearing what Betty Holcomb had gleaned.

A commotion in the hall caught her attention. Telling Betty she had to go, Delaney hurried across the room and opened the door just as a different transport team rolled Nick's gurney into the room. She fumbled to restore her mask. This was earlier than she'd expected.

"Thanks," one orderly said. "The door stuck."

Delaney motioned them in.

"Mommy," Nick mumbled when she rounded the rolling bed and took his hand. "Where's Daddy Dayo? He said he'd be here when I came back from the 'cedure."

"Procedure," Delaney stressed, leaning over the side rail to kiss him through her gauze mask. "I thought Dario was in the hallway. He only popped out to phone his brother, honey."

Two nurses swept into the room. Delaney had noticed that at this hospital the staff had defined jobs. The transport team didn't touch the patients, only delivered them to and from other sites. In the smaller facility where Nick had been throughout his first episode, jobs overlapped.

The nurses grabbed both edges of an under-sheet and deftly transferred Nick to his stationary bed. "Don't try to sit up, Nicky," a nurse cautioned. Turning to Delaney, she added, "He needs to lie flat for another hour at least. Otherwise he risks getting a horrible headache that could last for days."

Delaney bobbed her head. "I know. This isn't his first spinal tap. I'll be here to make sure he follows orders."

"As will I," Dario said from the doorway. He paused to right his mask.

"Daddy Dayo," Nick cried. "Come hold my hand." He shook loose from his mother, making her feel irrelevant for the second time in a short while.

"I'm hungry," Nick whispered when Dario stepped to the side of the bed to offer his hand. Dario first looked to the nurses, who were following the transport team out into the hall. So he turned his attention to Delaney. "I heard the nurse say he's not to sit up for a while. Does that mean he can't eat until later?"

"Good question," Delaney said, and caught up with the nurses at the door. "Nurse Trish," Delaney said, "may I give Nick a banana or something soft to eat if he lies on his side?"

"I'll see what's on the evening snack cart," Trish promised, pausing to smile at her patient. "Can you hold out a few minutes, Nick?"

"'Kay." Nick wrapped his small fingers around Dario's larger hand.

Once again Delaney felt like a fifth wheel. With Nick turned so he faced Dario, she had little choice but to go to the opposite side of the bed, which left her staring at her son's back. Was this what it felt like to coparent?

An aide came in a few minutes later carrying a tray that held a bottle of apple juice, a banana and something in a small covered dish. It looked like vanilla pudding. Approaching Dario, the woman handed him the tray, so he had to ease his hand out of Nick's death grip. "Hey, champ, let go, okay? I, uh, don't want to drop your food on the floor."

The aide didn't remain, leaving Dario to juggle the tray.

Taking pity on him, Delaney rounded the foot of the bed and righted the tray before all the food slid off.

"Daddy Dayo, I'm thirsty. But I need a straw. Mommy, is there one?"

"There is. No, don't lift your head." She switched the tray to her other hand and set her free palm on the side of Nick's head to keep him prone.

"I've no idea how one goes about eating or drinking in that position," Dario said. "This is a job for your mother, Nick. I'll sit here and watch, so I'll know how it's done."

Nick pouted, so Dario said, "How about if I hold the tray on my lap?"

"I guess so…"

Though crowded because Dario pulled his chair closer to the head of the bed, Delaney deftly opened the bottle of juice and angled the straw so the bendable tip was easy for Nick to reach. "Sip, don't gulp," she cautioned.

"Uh-oh, I dribbled." He tried to lick his chin.

"It's a good thing they gave us a couple of napkins." Dario unfurled one and reached around Delaney to tuck it under Nick's cheek.

"Thanks. Have you got other kids?" Nick peered at Dario through thick eyelashes.

"What? Ah, no." Dario shifted in his seat, plainly flustered by the question. "Uh, only you," he managed.

"Why? Don't you like kids? My friend Henry's got two brothers. He said they make him laugh."

"Well, I…uh…" Dario's fidgeting grew more pronounced, causing Delaney to stifle a smile.

"Henry was Nick's friend on his ward in Lubbock." She didn't want to add to Dario's obvious discomfort, but after all, he'd been the one to insist on getting to know his son. This was all a part of that process. "Nick, how about a bite of banana or a spoonful of pudding?" She knew the best way to distract a four-year-old was with food.

"Is it chocolate?"

"Vanilla." Again Delaney pressed his head down as he started to rise up to check out the pudding.

"Banana," he finally said after some hesitation.

Asking Dario to hold the juice, Delaney peeled part of the banana, and broke off a small chunk which she then held to Nick's lips.

The door swung inward again. This time Maria Sofia entered the room carrying her purse and three paper bags, a laptop clasped beneath her right arm. "Hey, what's up with you all being in a huddle? Oh, wait, let me grab a mask from the box outside the door."

Delaney knew Nick would automatically try to lift up to see the newcomer, so she had been prepared for Maria Sofia's return. She prevented him from moving with a gentle hand on his forehead. "Nick's supposed to lie prone a while longer, so he doesn't end up with a gorilla-sized headache."

Nick giggled around his second bite of banana.

Dario laughed, too. "Does Nick know monkeys, gorillas and boys all like bananas?"

"Yep, I've got a zoo book," Nick said proudly. "Mommy, where's my zoo book? I want Daddy Dayo to read it to me."

"We didn't bring all of your books, honey. It's probably still in your bookcase at home. If Zoey's family comes to visit again while you're still here, I'll see if they'll go by and get more of your books from Ms. Irene."

"Where will I be if I'm not here?" Nick squirmed, and frowned.

"I meant the Bannermans might not come to San Antonio again. When you get better, you and I will go back to La Mesa."

"Uh. With Daddy Dayo?"

Delaney stiffened, ready to say no, but she was stopped by Dario tugging on the back of her shirt sharply. Spinning around to scowl at him, she saw him shake his head.

"Let's first get you well, champ," he said evenly.

"'Kay." The boy reached for his stuffed cow, which always comforted him. "I don't want to eat any more, Mommy. It's too hard. When can I sit up?"

Delaney checked her watch. "We can ease you up with a pillow in half an hour. Why don't you drink some more juice?" Delaney took the bottle from Dario's hand.

"I don't want to go pee-pee in the bag the nurse said I hafta wear," he said, making a move as if to take it off. They heard the crinkle of plastic under his pajama bottoms.

She caught his hand. "I know you'd rather get up to go, Nick, but you don't want to have an accident."

"No, 'cause I'm a big boy now. When am I gonna get well?" His plaintive plea skewered Delaney through her heart. Her throat filled, and she couldn't find her voice.

Dario set the food tray on the bedside table. Scooting forward, he brushed the hair off Nick's forehead. "Dr. Von Claus said they're doing everything possible to make that happen, champ. Do you feel like playing tic-tac-toe on my phone like I showed you?"

The boy's eyes sparked in interest. "Can I play laying down?"

"Sure." Dario touched the screen to bring up the app and held the phone above Nick's face. "You start," he told Nick.

"Mommy, did you know me and Daddy Dayo are

both left-handed?" Nick asked as he chose the X and made the first mark.

Delaney didn't know. At least it hadn't registered. "Uh, no," she said feebly, thinking it was one more thing tying her son to Wonder Dad. Which was how Nick saw him.

Maria Sofia had remained quiet after unloading her stuff in the third chair. "Hey, I brought you guys sandwiches, remember?"

Dario gestured with his phone. "You and Delaney go on to the other side of the room and eat. In fact if you want to go down the hall and get coffee, feel free. My roast beef will still be good after the champ here and I play for half an hour. Maybe if I beat him he'll need part of my sandwich to pump his iron back up."

"I beat him last time we played," Nick bragged.

"So you did," Dario said, tucking his chin to his chest, acting like a man in defeat, coaxing a giggle from Nick.

Much as Delaney wanted Nickolas to choose her freely over Dario, she saw a bond between the two that couldn't be denied. Nor could she deny that Dario's explosion into Nick's life was a good thing, especially if he turned out to be the perfect donor.

Nick's doctor came swinging into the room. Dr. Von Claus always gave the appearance of a man in constant motion. "Nickolas, my little man. Your fever may be the result of a mild urinary infection. That also explains the pain you had in your tummy that I thought might be from a lymph gland." Turning to Delaney, he said, "We put an antibiotic in the drip he received in recovery. I've decided to go ahead and move him

to the ward in a couple of hours. I'll begin his experimental drug in the morning."

"Are other kids there?" Nick asked.

"Yes. A boy and girl your age and two a bit older.
All feel perky enough after a week on the drug to get
up and move about the ward. They're riding tricycles
around the room and that builds muscle. Does that
sound good to you?" The doctor listened to Nick's
lungs and took his pulse, nodding like he did when
he was satisfied.

"Can Daddy Dayo still visit me?"

"Of course. And your mother and aunt, too."

"Then I wanna go," Nick said.

The doctor turned to Delaney, who hovered at the
foot of Nick's bed. "You've had experience with his
erratic temps from the cancer, but urinary infections
aren't uncommon with kids confined to bed. I con-
sulted with a team urologist who, after looking at
Nick's lab tests, agreed with me. The sooner we get
him started on the trial drug so he feels like getting
up and about, the sooner his UTI will fade."

"Great. And if he goes to the ward tonight and settles in, I'll feel much better about being away from
him tomorrow for the donor recruitment."

"Good, good. Cells in bone marrow have a unique
ability to develop into many cell types, so the broader
the scope you get on the registry, the greater our
chance of finding someone with Nick's markers. I'll
go sign the order now to get him on the ward." Off he
sped, creating a breeze in his wake.

Still holding his phone at an angle allowing Nick to
see the tic-tac-toe grid, Dario asked Delaney, "I still
don't fully understand all I've heard about stem cells.

He's not saying a person's bone marrow cells are ever-changing, is he, Delaney?"

She shook her head. "No, they don't change from birth. Now I know that parents should spend whatever the cost to store their newborn's umbilical cord blood. It's the purest source of that child's stem cells. Had I done that, had the money or the foresight, we wouldn't be combing the population for a good match for Nick."

"But if cell types are inherited, why aren't you and I his best matches?"

"Because his makeup may have been drawn from us and either set of grandparents or great grandparents and so on. My dad was Welsh and Scottish, my mom English, Polish and German. You'd know some of your ancestors' bloodlines, but I doubt you know all. Dr. Avery explained to me that while you identify with your Spanish roots, many Argentineans have Italian or other core backgrounds."

"That's right. My maternal grandmother was born in France." He looked concerned. "How is a match ever found?"

"It's a melding of markers, Dario. Now you see why I want to go ahead with tomorrow's recruitment."

"That's smart," Maria Sofia said. "But worrying now isn't going to help anything. Why don't we pull our chairs over by the window and eat our sandwiches," she said, getting up to move her seat. "I'll show you the bulls Vicente chose for me to sell in Oklahoma."

"Chose for me, don't you mean?" Dario reminded her.

"I want to see the bulls," Nick chimed in. "I went with Mommy once when she had to give a big, big bull a shot. He roared and kicked. I was scared. 'Member that, Mommy? Tía, aren't you afraid to go sell those bad dudes?"

Her laughter tinkled through the room. "I'm only taking photographs of the animals to show prospective buyers, Nick. I'll let somebody else deliver the animals."

"But not you, Daddy Dayo?" The boy grabbed Dario's wrist, causing the man to gaze down into Nick's apprehensive brown eyes. At last, Dario slowly murmured, "No, son, I'm staying right here. Hey, let's finish our game. I think it's going to go to the cat. But you could pull it out and win."

"How do you tell who'll win before we're done?"

"Uh…it's something you learn the more you play."

"I don't wanna know. I'd rather wait and see."

Dario tossed back his head and laughed. "Smart kid. If you figure it out first, it takes a lot of fun out of playing."

Nick beamed. "Mommy, Daddy Dayo thinks I'm smart."

"And so you are. Don't I always call you precocious?"

"Uh-huh, but I didn't know that meant I'm smart."

They all chuckled over that, and a sense of congeniality settled over the adults as the women went across the room, unwrapped their sandwiches and the males finished their game and began another after Nick won, much to his delight.

"Okay, now that I've appeased my hunger pangs," Delaney said, "show me the bulls, Maria Sofia."

The younger woman set aside the uneaten half of her egg salad sandwich and opened the laptop. After hitting a few keys, she turned the device so Delaney could see the screen.

"Oh, a Brahma. Magnificent specimen. Brr," Delaney said, exaggerating a shiver.

"I wanna see," Nickolas called out, abandoning the game as he attempted to roll over.

"Hey, hey, champ. You still have some time to go before you sit up. Let them bring the laptop over so we can have a look."

Maria Sofia restored her mask and carried the laptop to Dario while Delaney did the same and moved behind him.

"Ah, Vicente chose well. *Toro Diablo*," Dario said, holding up the computer so Nick could see the black bull.

"Is that smoke coming from his nose?" Nick asked.

"Steam from his hot breath on a slightly chilly morning," Dario explained after taking a closer look. "I'm betting my brother Lorenzo's photography skills are showing the bull at his most provocative. Lorenzo would rather photograph bulls than work with them or sell them. You shouldn't have any problem selling this bull to a rodeo stockman. Let's see Vicente's second choice."

"He's not quite as scary-looking," Maria Sofia said, pulling up the next picture. "But his name, *Muy Malo*, means very bad, and he has the build of the Spanish fighting bulls."

"You know this how?" demanded Dario.

Nick touched the screen. "He's got a speckled bottom."

"That he does. He's a crossbreed. Am I wrong about

his fierceness for bucking?" Maria Sofia challenged her half brother.

"No." His answer was short.

Delaney set her hands on Dario's shoulders and leaned around him for a better look at the bull. "He does have the sleek, slanted hindquarters of a bull bred for the ring. You aren't doing that, are you? It's a disgusting practice."

Reaching up to clasp her hands, Dario dragged Delaney forward until the back of his head rested between her breasts.

His hair brushed her chin when he tried to look up at her. "Estancia Sanchez has a long and proud history, and we do not raise bulls for the ring. We sell to ranchers interested in improving the quality of their herds, and on occasion we market bucking bulls to rodeo stockmen."

Delaney's stomach cartwheeled from her close proximity to this man who himself reflected a proud history. Mesmerized by his growly voice, she couldn't see his expression well enough to read if he was angry or acting tough for show. *"Goood,"* she stammered, trying halfheartedly to twist loose. She didn't really want him to let go. She recognized factions that warred within her as being the love and longing she'd once felt for this man clashing with the humiliation she'd suffered at being abandoned by him.

Nick squirmed around on the bed. "Are you guys wrestling?"

Dario released Delaney at once.

Maria Sofia took her eyes off the computer screen. "Hey, you can do that after I go to present our package in Chickasha. You two will have the house to yourselves," she said with a wink. "Oh, but you haven't eaten, Dayo. And we still need to go over what's expected of us at the drive tomorrow."

Dario shrugged and got up. "I can't imagine it'll be too difficult. People who show up will have seen the flyer, right? If they don't speak English, well, we'll facilitate helping them fill out the form, yes?"

Still flustered by her close proximity to Dario, Delaney was slow to answer. Once she did, she held the back of his now-empty chair tightly. "It's funny, but people do drop by without knowing what the line-up is for. We'll be helped out by the local registry volunteers. And usually someone from a leukemia chapter will have pamphlets in English and Spanish to answer most-asked questions. We like to know that the people who sign up will, if called upon, try to follow through on being a donor. But we also don't pressure anyone. They have to sign up of their own free will."

"If they show up and get swabbed, why wouldn't they follow through?" Dario sounded genuinely surprised.

"A lot can get in the way. They may not be called for weeks or months or years. Maybe never. Life changes. People change. That's why it's so hard to keep a viable registry."

He nodded, then went to retrieve his roast beef sandwich.

"Nick, how about if I go find you some chocolate pudding?" Delaney said, straightening his sheet.

"Can I sit up now, and go to the bathroom?" He made a face. "Not in that yucky bag."

She checked her watch. "Yes, your time is up. Maybe Maria Sofia will track down chocolate pud-

ding at the nursing station while I help you. Sit up
slowly and dangle your feet a minute before you try
to stand and walk. And tell me if your back or your
head hurts, okay?"

He nodded and struggled to sit up.

Maria Sofia closed the computer, passed it to Dario
and started for the door. "Then can we go home, Dayo?
I'm so ready to use that beautiful pool."

"You go on. I'm staying." He picked up the car
keys she'd dropped on the table when she came in
with the food. He trailed her to the door, handed her
the keys and added, "I'll find the pudding. Go ahead,
take off now."

As Delaney helped Nick slowly toward the bathroom, she said, "There's no need for you to stick
around, Dario."

"Of course there is. It's not up for debate," he said,
a sharp edge to his voice.

Maria Sofia glanced from him to Delaney. Duck-
ing her head, she was about to leave when she said,
"Wait, I want the laptop." She darted back to get it.
"Oh…should I stick around, or are you going to walk?"

"Go on, it may be a while. It depends on when Nick
moves to the ward and whatever's entailed in making him comfortable. I'll catch a ride with Delaney."

From the doorway to the en suite bathroom, Delaney said, "I suppose I can drop you off. Anyway, I
should see where the house is." Opening the bathroom
door, she herded Nick in ahead of her. She bent to help
him, leaving the door ajar.

Dario continued talking to Maria Sofia. "I've been
thinking Delaney may as well swing past her motel
and gather her belongings. She can probably benefit

from a midnight swim, too. Her day has been fraught with worry. That way, we can go in one car to the recruiting event tomorrow."

"I heard that," Delaney called, sticking her head out of the little bathroom. "I don't need you making my decisions, Dario." Her tone was brusque.

"Mommy," Nick whined from beyond her. "Why are you and Daddy Dayo mad?"

"We're just having a discussion." Dario projected his voice so Nick would hear. "And now I'm going to track down chocolate pudding."

Delaney threw up her hands in defeat.

Dario dropped half of his mask and whistled on his way out the door.

Chapter Nine

Nick's transfer to his new ward was uneventful. When Delaney and Dario emerged from the hospital, the moon was bright in the sky. She breathed deeply, shrugged her shoulders then rotated her head. "I could go to my motel after I drop you," she said, "and worry about moving on Sunday."

"Why wait? I know you're tired, but you can't have much to move. Let's do it now." Stepping close behind her, he used his thumbs to loosen the tight muscles in her upper spine.

Releasing a kittenish purr, Delaney leaned into his massage. She heard a woman walking past them say to her partner, "Look, hon, there's a man who knows how to treat a woman."

Dario made a self-conscious choking sound. "Um, that's a little awkward," he muttered to Delaney, letting his hands slide off her shoulders.

"I don't know. I tend to agree with her. That felt heavenly. Okay, your massage has changed my mind. I'll check out of my motel tonight. Plus, Maria Sofia's promise of a relaxing, heated swimming pool sounds wonderful."

"Glad to hear you can be bribed." He followed her

to an aging, dusty SUV. He studied the vehicle criti-
cally. "This is what you drive? It looks older than some
of the knock-about vehicles we use out on our range."

"It has heart," Delaney said, unlocking his door
before getting in on the driver's side. "It belonged to
my dad," she said after the engine roared to life and
she backed out of the slot. "I was lucky it was so old at
the time his property had to be liquidated to pay bills.
The bank attorney didn't even list it on the manifest
of assets. I needed something with four-wheel drive
as I built my vet practice. Then after Nick was first
diagnosed with leukemia, I was lucky to have money
to keep this vehicle running."

"Another reason why you shouldn't have waited
five years to contact me."

"Dario, it's late and I'm too beat to argue with you
tonight. Our situation is what it is. I can't go back in
time and reverse decisions I made."

"Would you if you could?"

That question hit hard. "That's so not fair, Dario."

"Why?"

"You didn't keep any of the pretty promises you
made to me over that summer! To say nothing of what
you said during our night together."

"I didn't know I'd inadvertently left you with more
than promises, Delaney."

Unhappily, she swung along a row of cars outside
a garishly lit motel. She drove slowly past two levels
of identical orange doors, finally angling into an open
space in front of one. "Maybe you should call a cab to
take you back to your rental," she said. "Maybe sharing a house won't work if all we do is fight."

"Now that I've gotten a look at this dump, I wouldn't let you stay here on a bet."

"It's not that bad." She tried to sound convincing, but Dario uttered a rare expletive. Before he could climb out, a door on the level above Delaney's room flew open, and in the dim light they saw a woman shove a man out, after which she flung out clothing. A pair of jeans landed with a thud on Delaney's hood, and other items rained around the SUV.

Dario got out and plucked the jeans off the Jeep, tossing them to the ground. "I rest my case," he growled as he yanked open Delaney's door. "How fast can you pack?"

"It was cheap and it was near the hospital." Delaney sighed.

"And now you have a better option," Dario said, escorting her inside. The shouting on the balcony brought out other residents, none of whom were kind or quiet in their admonitions for the couple to shut up.

Inside her clean but modest room, Delaney collected her toothbrush and toiletries from the bathroom. She quickly folded a robe and shorty pajamas and added them to one of two small suitcases that remained mostly packed.

"Anything in the drawers?" Dario asked, watching her zip the larger bag.

She shook her head. "I didn't bring much. When Nick was admitted in Lubbock, it was near enough to La Mesa that I could drive home once a week to do laundry. I didn't have time to pack more when I returned from my whirlwind trip to Buenos Aires. I learned of the decision to move Nick to San Antonio while I was in the Miami airport. This is it," she said, hoisting her overnight bag to her shoulder. She bent to get the rolling case, only to have Dario relieve her of both.

"Do you need to leave the key card at the front office? Is there a front office?" He ducked to avoid a shirt floating down from the still-fighting couple above.

"I should. I'm paid up through Sunday," she said, opening the back. "Really, I'm glad to leave. Who knows how long that will go on?" Delaney rolled her head again and hunched her shoulders.

"Headache?" Dario inquired, taking in the grooves lining her forehead. "Would you like me to drive?"

She held the keys out, and he took them from her. They both kicked clothing aside. The poor guy upstairs was now being berated by more voices than that of the woman who had thrown him out.

Dario backed out, and stopped at the office so she could leave her key cards. He had cleared the complex parking lot by the time Delaney relaxed in her seat and closed her eyes. They rode in silence a while before she opened her eyes and straightened.

"That was less than a catnap," Dario said, giving her a smile.

"I was just resting. Hey, thanks for rescuing me. I've heard other, smaller commotions since renting there. None so near my room."

"I know you'll like the house. We're almost there."

"Really? This is an upscale neighborhood." She pressed her nose to the side window. "Big homes. Manicured lawns. Are you sure you didn't make a mistake when you figured the monthly costs?"

"Maria Sofia stumbled into a great deal." He explained the situation with Maria Sofia's professors. "It all works in our favor."

"I'll say."

Dario parked in the curved driveway behind his rental car. "I'll get your bags, if you want to go ring the bell and let Maria Sofia know it's us."

For the first time in five years, Delaney felt pampered. She reached for the doorbell, but Maria Sofia, with wet hair and wearing a colorful robe and slippers, opened the door first.

"I just stepped out of the shower when I heard your car drive in. Had a great swim! Did you get Nick moved?" she asked, beckoning Delaney in.

"We did. It's a big ward with other kids. His nearest neighbor is a sweet six-year-old girl named Heather. She's a chatterbox like Nick. I figure it'll be a toss-up as to who talks whose ear off first. They both waved us off as if we were in their way."

Dario came in with Delaney's bags and joined the conversation. "For sure, neither of those kids is shy," he said. "I think it hurt Delaney's feelings when Nick dismissed us as fast as he did."

"Well, it does hurt when you go from being the big cheese in your child's life to set aside for strangers." She eyed him pointedly.

"Kids are fickle." Dario's voice sounded muffled from the bedroom. He emerged, saying, "I set your bags on the bed, Delaney. Do you want to change and go for a swim right now, or unpack first?"

Suddenly, she realized what wasn't in her bags. "Yikes, I'll have to forego a swim. I don't know why it didn't occur to me before, but I don't have a suit. Swimming isn't a pastime I indulged in even at home."

Dario's eyes lit with mischief. "Hey, I could be arm-twisted into skinny-dipping."

His sister, who stood nearest to him, smacked his arm. "I brought extra suits. I love to swim, and I knew any hotel we stayed at would have a pool. Two are like new. I'll get them, and you can take your pick." She rushed off into an adjacent room and soon returned dangling four scraps of material for Delaney's perusal. One bikini was black with white piping, the other a blue-green Hawaiian print.

"Mercy." Delaney sounded strangled for air. "I... ah...think I'll shower and skip swimming."

"Coward," Dario chided.

"The pool is heated," Maria Sofia said. "The dark aqua in this one matches your eyes, Delaney."

She took the suit. "Thanks. Maybe I'll blend in with the water. Calling someone a coward is like challenging her to a duel," she told Dario before marching into the room where he'd deposited her suitcases.

The door slammed behind her.

"Where's my gentlemanly brother?" Maria Sofia demanded, hands on her hips. "That was a beastly remark," she said, her British accent pronounced. "Don't you dare wolf whistle when she comes out, Dario."

He pretended to act contrite, but he couldn't stop his purely male snicker. "I'll go change. And I need to finalize my Oklahoma trip...uh, your trip. I got you an early flight out Sunday, returning Thursday. I'll get the stockman's information from Vicente. Tomorrow, between recruiting donors, you can arrange a hotel and where to meet the customer." Dario ran a hand through his hair. "Do you know the reservations I have about you handling this sale?"

"I promise I won't let you down."

"I should probably have my head examined," he said before disappearing into his room.

Delaney peeked out and exited her room in time to hear the last exchange. She was wrapped in a big bath towel that covered her from chest to knees. "What's he grumbling about now?"

"My going off to sell bulls." The girl ran a brush she carried through her drying hair. "Come on, I'll show you where to turn on the underwater pool lights. There are lights on the patio, but they attracted bugs. Dayo went to change and phone Vicente. You may have plenty of time to swim before he finishes that phone call. Papa and Vicente want us home."

"Surely not before we get his HLA results?" Delaney padded barefoot after Maria Sofia.

"Don't worry. There's no way he'd go now. Even when that time does come, Dayo's going to be in a quandary."

"What do you mean? If he's a match he'll receive injections for five days of a drug called filgrastim designed to increase the number of blood-forming cells in his bloodstream. Once the doctor draws liquid marrow from the back of his pelvic bone, he should be fine to fly back to Argentina."

After throwing the switch turning on the pool lights, Maria Sofia paused. "Don't you know how torn up over leaving Dayo will be? Nick is his son." She leveled a long look at Delaney, then slipped back inside, leaving Delaney alone on the patio.

She shivered. No two ways about it, Nickolas *was* Dario's son. But, what exactly did it mean, him being torn about going home? Feeling her head begin to hammer again, and not wanting to think about how she might fare in a custody battle with Dario, she shed her towel on the edge of the pool and slid into the warm water.

When Dario came out from the house, he watched Delaney aimlessly floating on her back. There was just enough light to cause his heart and other parts of him to ache. She looked so alluring in that bikini. Maybe he wanted her all the more because he was still steamed after the go-round he'd had with his father and brother. Both men insisted he owed his allegiance to *la familia*. The pair had cut off all of his attempts to say Nick was family. Dario didn't like being ganged up on. It wasn't as if he didn't realize how falling hard and fast for a foreigner had caused problems in the family business. But that was done. Like Delaney had said earlier, they couldn't undo their past. If truth be known, he didn't want to. And if they'd quit deleting the cell phone photos he sent of his son, Papa and Vicente would see why he couldn't go back to the way things were before Delaney had paid him that shocking visit.

Through narrowed eyes Delaney surreptitiously watched Dario study her after shedding his robe. She would have sunk from self-consciousness if not for the fact his face was lined with worry. He stood in one place so long after disrobing that she finally righted herself, and she spoke as she treaded water. "Are you going to stand there all night, or stick your big toe in? I'll vouch for the fact it's every bit as relaxing as Maria Sofia told us."

Startled by her addressing him, he jumped in with a big splash that washed Delaney into deeper water.

She sputtered and came up coughing.

"Sorry." Dario swam close. "Do you need a towel? I didn't mean to swamp you."

"I brought it on myself by teasing you." She wiped away big droplets clumped together on her eyelashes. "You looked so serious. Is everything okay at home? You were talking to Vicente, right?"

Dario drifted a foot or so away from her into the deeper part of the pool. He lazily kicked his feet to remain in place. "You looked asleep. I worried that you'd slip under and drown."

"Hmm. If you don't want to tell me what was on your mind, that's fine."

"You want me to admit I'm admiring you in a bikini?"

Delaney cupped her hands together and threw a huge scoop of water over him.

He merely laughed and shook the hair out of his eyes, which gleamed mischievously in the diffused light. Breaststroking right up to her so their arms touched, he sobered and said, "I'll admit my family is difficult."

"You didn't tell Vicente that Maria Sofia is going to sell the bulls, did you?"

"No, my time was spent trying to make them understand I'm not staying in San Antonio out of a misguided sense of duty. They won't listen, and they ignore me when I tell them Nick matters. Papa actually expects—because he thinks I'm going on the sales trip to Oklahoma—that a separation from you and Nick will make me come to my senses."

Maybe because she felt so relaxed, Delaney decided to press Dario on the issue that had been hanging over her like a sword. "I know you aren't going to

Oklahoma, and frankly, I've shied away from asking before, but I have to know. What are your long-term intentions toward Nick?"

All at once she felt pinned by Dario's steady gaze and became aware of heat growing in the spots where their bare, wet skin brushed. For an excruciating moment they drifted in silence, leaving her to wonder if she'd messed up by asking.

"I wish I knew for sure," he finally said. "It probably looks to you as if I'm happy operating day-to-day. When I got here I was full of skepticism. Then I met Nick and, well, the only way I can describe it is…all my doubts evaporated." Wrapping his hands around Delaney's upper arms, he maneuvered them into the shallow end so they could both stand. "Nick lights up when he greets me. And when he calls out 'Daddy Dayo,' I feel ten feet tall. I'm hit with a flash of…seeing him grow…helping him grow up. Then the truth of our situation along with his condition intrudes and I get frustrated. Tell me, how do you picture my long-term role?"

"I c-can't." She averted her eyes. "More than anything I want you to be the perfect donor for Nick. I want the marrow transplant process to be successful for you and him. I rarely let myself dream into the future. You and I both have established lives and jobs in separate parts of the world." She offered a helpless shrug.

"Yeah, and for Nick, that's a bitch."

"What do you mean?" Delaney jerked her eyes back to Dario. She was terrified what his statement hinted at, that he would demand half of Nick's time.

Expression anguished, Dario only ran his hands up and down her arms, pulling her close.

Delaney felt the slam of both of their hearts against each other's chest as his grip tightened. The last thing she expected, given the conversation they'd been having, was for him to yank her up on her toes and kiss her with a desperate grinding of his lips on hers. She fluttered one hand on his water-slick chest. Above them a big golden moon looked as if someone had taken a bite out of it. And as Dario nipped at her lips, her chin and her neck below her ear, she wanted to take a big bite out of him. Lifted off her feet, she felt the swell of his erection nudge her lower abdomen, and the bones in her legs turned weak. A tiny part of her brain said they should stop this even as she circled his neck with both arms and feverishly returned his kisses. The fact was he had the same effect on her now as he'd had five years ago.

From a distance, a voice shouting Dayo's name shattered Delaney's attempt to get much closer to him in this moment of moon madness. For what else could she call what was happening? Panting, she wrenched loose. "Maria Sofia is calling you," she mumbled through kiss-numbed lips that tasted faintly of chlorine. Gathering her wits, Delaney forced her unsteady limbs to carry her to the side of the pool. Sheer force of will allowed her to hoist herself up on the cool deck near where she'd left her towel. She wrapped herself within its thick folds before Dario even turned and responded to his sister.

"What's so urgent?" he asked in a low, annoyed voice.

"Vicente's on the phone. Apparently a rodeo stockman in New Mexico heard a representative from Estancia Sanchez is peddling bucking bulls in the United States. The man wants you...well, me, to add on a day to meet with him. Vicente said the guy will pick up the tab for the extra hotel costs and flight changes. I tried to get all of the information, but our dear brother will only impart that to you."

Dario threw up his hands and sloshed half the length of the pool to a set of steps. He climbed out and snatched his terry cloth robe from the back of the chair.

Delaney got up and tried to scoot past Maria Sofia without notice. But the girl swung around. "Did I break up another argument?" she asked. "If so, good. You guys were supposed to make nice and let the warm water sooth away your cares and woes. Aren't those the words in some old American song?"

Because she couldn't be irritated at Maria Sofia, Delaney gave her a spontaneous hug. "The water was lovely."

"Yes, it was."

Delaney jumped, not realizing Dario was so close behind her left shoulder. She hurriedly went back inside and escaped into her room.

DARIO STARTED TO follow her, then said to Maria Sofia, "Where's the phone?"

"When Vicente couldn't get you, he called on my cell. I said you'd phone him back. I didn't say you were in the pool fighting with Delaney. He would have been overjoyed."

"Did Delaney say we were fighting?"

"No, but I'm no dummy. Your body language and hers radiated tension."

"Who taught you about body language? The nuns?"

"As a matter of fact, yes. Sister Mary Rose from Italy was young and quite progressive."

Dario opened his mouth to pop off a reply, thought better of it and said instead, "Will you shut off the pool lights while I deal with Vicente?"

"Okay, but I want to do both jobs, Dayo. If I close one sale, he and Papa can say it's a fluke. If I handle two, they'll have to consider letting me take over for Lorenzo. Won't they?"

Already through the door, Dario stomped down the hall, pretending not to hear her. He should put his foot down and tell Vicente there would be no side trip— period. But he was beginning to wonder if the relationship that had once burned hot between him and Delaney could be salvaged. There was still chemistry between them, and he'd like to explore further. Lasting relationships had probably developed on less than chemistry and a shared child. But hanging over his desire to have more alone time with Delaney was a real worry about sending Maria Sofia to do a job his family expected him to do. And in spite of her insistence that she had what it took to sell their animals, he was fully aware of what their papa would say. He'd catch hell if anything went wrong, and he'd deserve it. Still, that didn't mean he liked Vicente forcing him to make choices between the *estancia* and Nick. Flopping down in a big rocking chair, he turned on the lamp and picked up his phone. He redialed and gazed at the ceiling until his brother came on the line, growling in Spanish that it was about damned time Dario called back.

A burning sensation started in the middle of Dario's

chest and spread, causing him to retort, "Screw you, too, Vicente. Arrange for the damned meeting in Albuquerque. Text me the info. But no more, do you hear? I am not at your beck and call. I'm in Texas because my son is sick. He's family, Vicente. Get used to it." Clicking off, Dario threw the phone down on his nightstand and went to the en suite bathroom to shower, aware that the phone buzzed repeatedly until his brother finally gave up. *Too bad.* Vicente often forgot Dario was an equal partner in the *estancia*.

That *could* change. So perhaps that was the prospect he should explore before he allowed old feelings for Delaney to bubble up and cloud reason as he'd let happen five years ago. Which wasn't to deny that those old feelings still existed. Oh, no, they definitely still existed.

Chapter Ten

Delaney jerked awake to the *ding, ding, ding* of her cell phone alarm. It took her several seconds to assimilate the unfamiliar surroundings. When she connected the soft bed and lovely room decor with the happy sound of birds chirping outside her window, she remembered where she was and shut off the alarm. Sitting up and stretching, she had to admit that that had been the most restful night's sleep she'd had in months. Taking another lazy minute to just savor that fact, she then tried to figure out why she felt so good. Was it because she knew Nick wasn't stuck in a room by himself, or because she had companions in the house? *Dario Sanchez, for one.* Should she credit his amorous send-off to beddy-bye last night for this warm sense of well-being?

Remembering the passion he evoked brought heat to her cheeks. She had to admit that it had been a lovely interlude. It had been so long since anyone had just held her. But did his kiss mean anything, or had it happened due to ambiance and her proximity? And more importantly, did she want it to be significant? Did she want to let go and allow it to happen again?

It was a debate that raged inside her head while she

straightened her bed and got dressed for the donor re-cruitment.

She had almost finished braiding her hair when there was a sharp rap at her door.

"Are you up?" Maria Sofia's sweet voice rang out.

Delaney left the en suite bathroom to open the outer door. "I'm nearly ready to face the day." She checked her watch. "We have a couple of hours until we're scheduled to meet the coordinator from the local donor bank."

"Yes, but I wanted to let you know that Dayo ran to the grocery store. We thought we'd have coffee, scrambled eggs and toast this morning. You guys can pick up more supplies after I leave for Oklahoma."

"Sure enough. Sorry, my brain is still asleep. It's been months since I've slept in such a heavenly bed."

"It sure feels more like home than it did at the hotel. I told Dayo it's too bad the place didn't come with a cook and maid service, though." The girl made a face.

"Since I've never had either, I was delighted to see a dishwasher in the kitchen. I assume there's a coffee-maker and pots and pans. Shall we go see?"

They were in the kitchen when Dario whipped in, bringing sacks of groceries and a breath of fresh air. He looked so appealingly masculine, Delaney's breath caught.

"I see you found a coffeemaker," he said. "I bought travel mugs so we can carry coffee with us."

"I hope we have time to run by the hospital to see Nick." Again Delaney glanced at her watch. She im-mediately set to work unloading and putting away the groceries.

"If we go quickly, I figure we'll have fifteen or

twenty minutes to visit him. To be sure, I picked up packets of sugar and powdered creamer. I drink my coffee black. I don't know how you take yours, Delaney."

"The same," she mumbled even as she felt some of her earlier anticipation about rekindling their relationship fade. They'd made a son together, but neither of them knew something as simple about the other as how each took their coffee. Good, long-lasting marriages weren't built on a few weeks of flirting and one night of steamy sex. Relationships took sharing hopes and dreams, and intimately learning mundane details about each other.

"How do you take yours, Maria Sofia?" she asked, to deflect her fears.

"Oh, she sweetens hers, in hopes it'll improve her disposition," Dario teased.

He darted away so his sister missed when she tried to smack him.

"Children!" Delaney inserted herself between them and handed Maria Sofia cinnamon bread to toast. "You two put me in mind of the squabbles that used to go on between my babysitter's granddaughter and Nickolas when he was well."

"Sibling rivalry is healthy," Dario said lightly, eyeing Delaney as she cracked eggs in a bowl and began to beat them with a fork. "You missed out by being an only child."

She arched an eyebrow at him. "Fighting is not good."

Maria Sofia grimaced. "For sure, not if you're the youngest."

Dario burst out laughing. "Oh, right. Like Papa

didn't dream up dastardly chores if any of we three boys so much as raised our voice at you."

"We've outgrown that," Maria Sofia assured Delaney. "And for every time one of them picked on me, many more times they banded together to watch out for me. You'll see how it works when you give Nick a little sister."

Delaney's egg beating faltered.

"You want more kids, don't you?" The girl slid in the question as she passed Delaney a skillet she'd sprayed with cooking oil.

Dario leaned forward as if waiting for her answer. His interest made Delaney's hand shake as she warmed the pan over the gas flame and poured in the eggs. "So much would have to change in my life for that question to be relevant," she said, turning down the flame.

"But you're not opposed?" Dario asked. He took out three plates from the cupboard while his sister put cinnamon bread in the toaster. Then he froze. "Wait, I've never asked if blood cancer like Nick's came from us."

"There are studies underway looking at DNA mutations. I've read up on the subject. Most specialists believe it's random. Nick's doctors believe that."

The toaster popped. Delaney shut off the gas and separated the fluffy eggs on to three plates. Maria Sofia placed a slice of buttered toast atop the eggs, then helped Delaney carry the plates to the table.

Dario poured coffee before the maker finished perking.

"Do you say grace?" Maria Sofia asked. "At home, Papa insists on it. And at school the Sisters offered a blessing before every meal. Dayo?"

"I'm fine skipping it."

"I haven't raised Nick Catholic," Delaney blurted.

"It's not too late." Maria Sofia gestured with her fork. "It will matter to Papa."

Squeezing her cup, Delaney fixed Dario with a stubborn gaze. "My sitter is a devout Baptist. When I worked on Sunday, which I often do, Nick attended church with Irene and her family."

"Your sitter doesn't live in?" Dario asked after taking a slug of coffee.

"No, down the street. She watches Nick and her granddaughter. Irene is wonderful. Nick will be lost next year when Sara Beth, her granddaughter, starts kindergarten. But maybe she'll take in another child. Or, who knows? My life could change totally by then."

Dario fiddled with his cup. "I should have asked earlier if you're dating anyone seriously."

Delaney frowned and said, "I guess you have a right to ask if Nick's going to have a stepfather. No, I'm not seeing anyone. I didn't mean my life would change like that. I meant I could lose my current clients to the vets covering for me, and have to start anew someplace else." She could have told him she'd only dated a handful of times since Dario abandoned her, but that would sound pathetic.

Talk fell off as they ate and cleaned up dishes. Dario filled the new travel mugs with the remaining coffee and tossed his sister a baggy filled with sugar packets. Then they all trooped out to Dario's rental. Maria Sofia started to climb in back, but Delaney stayed her. "You take the front seat."

The girl hesitated, but then climbed in front.

They'd almost reached the hospital when Delaney

noticed Dario kept glancing at her in his rearview mirror. "Is something wrong?" she finally asked.

"Uh, no. You fixed your hair different today. I like it."

"Thanks." She felt her neck and face grow warm. "I wear it braided a lot when I work. It stays put when I bend or stretch to examine a horse or cow."

"Ah…well, our vet is a gruff old bald guy."

His sister reached across the seat and poked him. "I think Dayo's trying to say he'd like it if you were our vet. But then our vet bills would go up and productivity down, because all our bull handlers would manufacture problems so they could watch you bend and stretch."

Delaney gave a self-conscious laugh. "I might be a curiosity for one visit, but I can assure you that's gone once a rancher gets my bill. They quickly realize I'm a necessary evil."

Grinning, Dario parked and they all got out and went into the hospital. On the elevator he sidled in next to Delaney. Stopping outside the door to Nick's ward, Maria Sofia asked, "Should we all go in at once? Hey, no box of masks out here." She sounded hesitant.

"The nurse said sometimes they require masks. When they do, a box will be attached to the door. And today we're only staying a minute." Delaney slipped into the ward. Very few of the kids were in bed. Most sat at a low table eating breakfast, except for an older girl in a wheelchair with a tray.

"Mommy!" Nick broke off talking to another child to wave a greeting with his spoon. "Where's Daddy Dayo? And Tía? These are all my new friends. I got my first jumping-juice medicine this morning."

"Really?" Delaney walked over and dropped a kiss on Nick's dark curls. A boy seated across from him of about seven or eight spoke up.

"That's what Dr. Von Claus calls the medicine we all take. It's s'posed to give us pep. Most of us have been here a few weeks."

"Do you feel a difference?" Dario asked as he ambled up and ruffled Nick's hair.

"Ev'rybody, this is my daddy. He comed here from another planet."

"Whoa, whoa," Dario said. "It's another continent, Nick, my man."

The older kids all guffawed but didn't tease Nickolas too badly. The girl with no hair and huge blue eyes that Delaney and Dario had met the night before said softly, "You're lucky your family is all here, Nick. My dad works on an oil rig, and Mama can only visit some weekends 'cause I've got a baby sister, and my big brother's in school."

That threw a damper on the kids for a minute until Nick said, "But, Heather, the doctor said you got a donor. Daddy Dayo, Mommy and Tía hafta go today to see if they can find me one. You'll get better and go home and go to school." Nick sighed.

The girl blotted her tears. "I've been sick a long time. I'm afraid kids at school will laugh 'cause I don't have hair."

Delaney knelt beside her. "Heather, you are beautiful and your hair will grow back." She hugged the girl before she rose. Her assertion had been enough for all of the others to second her assurance.

Dario gazed at Delaney with open admiration.

Maria Sofia inclined her head, indicating they needed to go.

"We have to take off now, Nick," Dario said. "We'll stop back after we sign up all of the prospective donors."

Nick held up his arms for a hug, which triggered a warm rush of emotion in Delaney.

No one said anything until they stopped to wait for the elevator. "I almost bawled back there, Delaney," Maria Sofia said. "Some of these kids have it hard. I want to buy Heather a cute head scarf or a colorful floppy hat. I hate to think anyone will laugh at her. It's just wrong."

Delaney entered the nearly empty elevator. "I thought I'd gotten thick-skinned having seen so many really sick children during Nick's first bout. Heather, at least, has hope. Did you see the faces of some of the other kids? At four, Nick assumes he'll get well. Some of the older kids have real doubts. Many have probably lost friends they met in treatment." Her shoulders bowed, and Dario rubbed her neck until they reached the lobby. Delaney could tell by how quiet he was that the exchange had shaken him, too.

"After my mom died I swore I'd live each day to the fullest," Maria Sofia said. "I'm never taking good health for granted. Nick will get a donor, you guys."

Dario unlocked the car. He got in after helping the women settle in. "How long do you think it'll be before we get the results of my test?"

Delaney shrugged. "They say three weeks, but mine came back sooner. I guess a lot depends on how busy the lab is."

"I'm not good with waiting."

"I'll attest to that," Maria Sofia said around a low chuckle. "Impatience, thy name is Dayo."

"Smart aleck!"

Delaney tapped his shoulder. "Take a left at the next street. The park fans out at the end of the block."

He followed her directions to a small but fairly full parking lot.

His sister pointed to his left. "There's a van with the Marrow Donor logo on its side."

Delaney leaned between them. "I see the table where they've set up. They look busy. Gosh, I'm so relieved. People are already filling out forms."

"Didn't you expect people to show up?" Dario asked once he'd parked.

"I wasn't sure. We're strangers here. I know from experience the odds are less than stellar. Jill listed our need to attract Latino donors on the flyer, though."

As they headed for the test site, Maria Sofia pointed to a light pole on which someone had taped Delaney's flyer. "That photo is adorable. How could anyone resist helping a cute kid with that gap-toothed grin?"

Dario stopped to inspect the flyer. He cleared his throat a few times as he trailed a finger over the likeness of mother and son. "He's smiling, but he looks pale, and his eyes don't sparkle."

Delaney hadn't stopped, but Maria Sofia slipped an arm around her brother's waist and for a moment leaned her head on his shoulder. "Keep the faith," she murmured.

"I'm trying, but it's hard. We're in limbo until he gets a marrow transplant."

"Will you be any less in limbo then? I didn't tell you Papa phoned last night. He ordered me to distract you from getting too involved with Delaney and Nick. I'm supposed to persuade you to escort me to Dallas and Austin on the pretext of clothes shopping." She rolled her eyes. "Neither Papa nor Vicente get the message that it's too late to wrest you away. I wonder, Dayo, has it totally sunk in with you?" She trotted off after Delaney, leaving Dario rooted in front of the flyer.

OH, HE KNEW. His last barrier had fallen last night. He'd stayed awake a long time plotting what to do. But Delaney remained the wild card. Her apprehension when it came to co-parenting Nick couldn't be more obvious. He could better lay her fears to rest once his test came back proving he was the right donor. Until then he'd bide his time and further explore his options. One plan in particular seemed promising...

Seeing the women beckoning him, he hurried off in their direction, but promised himself when this event was over he'd swipe that flyer and fax a copy to the *estancia*. Only an unfeeling cynic wouldn't see the Sanchez family resemblance in Nick. His dad and brother could be stubborn, but he didn't think either one of them was totally hard-hearted.

"What's up?" he asked at large on joining the group.

Delaney introduced him to Sue Hardesty and Louise Jenkins, the donor coordinator and nurse volunteer for the event. "They are delighted to see you, Dario. Sue says, often men are wary of drives like this, not as easily convinced to be tested as their wives or girlfriends are. She hopes having you explain our purpose in Spanish may entice some men who otherwise would opt out."

"Oh, boy. No pressure."

"There isn't any really, Dario. We explain what we're doing and underscore the need, but we don't break kneecaps."

"Glad to hear it. For a minute you had me worried." Then, because she looked so serious but so attractive, Dario kissed the tip of her freckled nose.

She covered the spot with her hand and hissed, "Stop. Why did you kiss me?"

"I felt like it. And if we don't get busy helping out here, I'm gonna be tempted to kiss you again."

"Don't. We have serious work to do. Even if you end up being Nick's match, there are thousands of other kids who need a marrow transplant."

"Okay, that's sobering. Explain what I need to do."

They went to the table where the women from the local registry explained the setup. Louise was the volunteer nurse who did the cheek swabs. "The writing, especially on the strip we tear off and wrap around the test tube, needs to be legible. Offer to help if you can't decipher a potential donor's handwriting."

Each of them staked out their place at the table, helping process the steady stream of residents who began stopping by. Some only wanted to see what was going on. A few asked questions and took brochures, promising to think about donating. And there were people who asked how to help fund the work. The day flew by at warp speed.

No one got lunch.

Later, the sun slipped behind a copse of trees and their lines petered out. Finally even the family whose children were playing on the swings and slides went away.

Sue Hardesty was the first to suggest they wind

things down. "Lou just counted our specimens. We logged a hundred-and-two swabs today. Thank you, everyone. I can't think when I've held a more productive roundup. I credit you, Dr. Blair. Your flyers were professional, and your Spanish-speaking crew made a huge difference."

Delaney watched Louise secure the lid to the cooler holding the swabs. "I'm happy to help. I know firsthand how important the National Bank is."

"How soon will these samples be processed and put on the larger registry?" Dario asked.

"Barring problems, a couple of weeks." Sue paused as she fit leftover forms into her briefcase. "You know that's only step one. If a sample is found to be compatible, it kicks off more tests. Unfortunately some people, who had the test today will back out when the rubber meets the road. It was kind of you to come out to help Dr. Blair's son, Dario."

"Nickolas is *our* son," Dario stressed, settling his hand on Delaney's shoulder.

"I...I'm sorry, I didn't realize," Sue stammered.

Delaney stood by speechless. She felt hot, then cold, then hot again. Who would've thought two little words could pack such a wallop? *Our son.* Even though she'd finally admitted to herself that he had the right to call Nick his son, she always thought of Nickolas as *my son.* She'd never let the term *ours* invade her mind. A few uncomfortable moments passed, but she managed to gather her wits and respond, "No need for apology, Sue. I wasn't clear when I introduced Dario and his sister."

The awkwardness dissipated thanks to Dario, who

picked up the cooler Louise was about to lift. "Here, let me carry that to your van."

Maria Sofia further glossed over the moment, saying, "I'm famished. I hope we're going to get something to eat now."

"We did work right through lunch," Delaney agreed. "I'd like to go to the hospital, though. I get anxious spending this much time away from Nick."

"I'm sure he's fine," Maria Sofia said.

"I know we told him this morning it'd probably be late before we got back to see him, and he acted happy to be among kids. But time doesn't always make sense to a four-year-old."

Maria Sofia fell in beside Delaney as they trekked to the parking area. "This morning I heard that little girl Heather say her parents didn't get to visit her very often. How are you able to take so much time away from work?"

Dario, who walked ahead of them between Sue and Louise, turned to them. "Maria Sofia, I know you were raised with better manners than to ask such a personal question."

"What did I do that's so wrong?" She screwed up her face.

"It's okay," Delaney assured the girl. "I'm lucky to have grown up in a close-knit community, and now I work in that community. Local ranchers and other friends set up a fund for Nickolas. They were very generous, and I'll never be able to repay their kindness. But the fund isn't bottomless. I can't take off forever, but I can't imagine leaving Nick alone to work while he's this far away." She rubbed a thumb between her eyebrows. "We need a donor soon."

"There's going to be one," Dario asserted. "Me." He set the cooler in the back of Louise's van, and they all said their goodbyes.

In their car again, Dario asked, "Did we decide to eat in the hospital cafeteria?"

"I'm okay with it," Maria Sofia said. "I know Delaney is eager to check on Nick."

"Definitely."

Dario started the car and followed the van out to the main street. Sue Hardesty turned left toward downtown. Dario went right in the direction of the hospital. "Delaney," he began as the huge hospital complex came into sight, "I'm glad to hear you've had financial help, but are you bogged down by medical bills?"

Maria Sofia glanced up from a text she was typing into her smart phone. "This question from the man who insinuated it was crass of me to bring up money?"

Dario shot her a dark look. "You brought it up around strangers. We're family." To Delaney, he said, "I have savings. I'm ready to help if you need it, Delaney."

"I appreciate the offer, but my insurance covered us last time. And I'll be forever indebted to Dr. Avery. He arranged for Nick to join Dr. Von Claus's study. It covers all costs except his transportation to San Antonio. I paid that from Nick's fund. Also for my trip to Argentina, and so far my expenses here. The two vets covering my practice pay me a percentage, which so far pays my lease—my home is attached to my clinic.

Delaney was grateful to see they'd reached the hospital. Discussing money with Dario made her uncomfortable. She knew that was petty, and that she should stop thinking of him as the enemy. But some part of her remained wary of falling under his spell again.

Maria Sofia stopped right inside the lobby doors. "I'm going directly to the cafeteria."

"I'll come down after I check on Nick," Delaney said.

Dario placed his hand on Delaney's waist. "Same for me."

Delaney had to admit that Dario's warm hand was comforting, but it also sparked a familiar heat inside her. It would be so easy to succumb.

At the door to the ward, they were stopped by an exiting nurse. "Oh, Dr. Blair and Mr. Sanchez, I'm glad I caught you. Nick has been in bed all afternoon. He'll seem extra tired. Dr. Von Claus asked me to tell you that it's a good sign. His first dose from last night boosted his energy like we hoped. He wore himself out from being so active and playing with the other children. Not all the kids have had positive results with the first dose like Nick did."

Delaney and Dario hung on her every word. "Should we stay, or go and let him catch up on sleep?" Delaney asked.

"Your choice," the nurse said, "but he probably won't be very responsive. Just know his lethargy isn't a setback."

Delaney went in first. None of the kids on the ward appeared as energetic as they had been earlier. Curtains were half pulled around the head of Nick's bed. He slept curled around his stuffed cow. She feathered a kiss across his forehead, but all he did was snuggle closer to his toy.

Opposite her, Dario stroked a finger over Nick's

small hand. His gentle expression sent a corkscrew of yearning through Delaney.

Heather was in the next bed, watching a TV mounted on the wall. "Nickolas is okay," she whispered. "The medicine fired him up, but that's good."

"Yeah," said an older boy from across the room. "Dr. Von Claus says the first dose acts like a spark plug."

Nodding, Delaney said, "I think we won't wake him. Heather, will you be sure he knows his father and I came by?"

"Sure. Where's the pretty blonde lady who was with you at breakfast?"

"Downstairs in the cafeteria. We all missed lunch," Dario said, "so we're about to join her."

The girl nodded. "Nickolas is lucky. You're all so nice."

As they left, they met Maria Sofia in the hall. "Hey, are you finished eating already?" Delaney asked.

"I wanted to get Nick's neighbor a cute hat first. I found two in the gift shop that I like a lot, so I'm taking them to her now. Why are you leaving Nick so soon?"

Dario explained.

"Heather asked about you," Delaney added.

"She called you a pretty blonde lady." He tweaked his sister's curls.

"Smart kid. Hey, will you order me a naked taco salad while I run in and see how Heather likes these?"

Sharing a confused look, Delaney and Dario asked in unison, "What's a naked taco salad?"

"One without meat. The other day I asked if they could make a taco salad without hamburger or chicken, and the woman at the salad bar said that's what I should ask for."

Dario gave her a thumbs-up. "Got it. Or…we could wait in the car. Since it's early, we could fix a meal at home."

"Sounds good to me," said Delaney.

"Me, too. Plus, my flight leaves at ten tomorrow," Maria Sofia reminded them. "I only packed a few essentials last night. Going home to eat suits me."

After riding to the lobby, Delaney and Dario walked out to the car. They stood beside it a moment, both admiring the vivid colors in the sunset.

"How gorgeous. I never tire of our Texas sunsets." Delaney let out her breath in a slow exhale. After a few moments, she said to Dario, "Hey, you're quiet all of a sudden."

"Am I doing the right thing, letting Maria Sofia make this sales trip?"

"You said she could go. It would be wrong to deny her the opportunity now. You could go along, but she'd resent it forever."

"You're right." He leaned against the car and pulled her tight against his body, skimming a finger down her nose. He laughed when she wrinkled the bridge. "Have you considered how her trip will give us a few days alone? It's our opportunity to discuss the future."

Delaney wiggled away and rubbed at a sudden chill that traveled up both arms. "I'm not prepared to have that talk until Nick gets a donor and is on the path to recovery."

When Dario didn't say anything, she glanced over her shoulder and was surprised to see hurt in his eyes. "I really am glad that you're here," she said, then bit down hard on her bottom lip. After having touched base again with the legal adviser, she'd learned from

Betty Holcomb that custody could get dicey in a country with patriarchal laws. That still frightened her.

Dario cupped her chin. "Being glad I'm here is a start," he said, and looked ready to say more, but Maria Sofia appeared beside them.

"Next stop—home," she announced. "I'm so hungry I could eat a horse, and that ought to tell you I'm starving."

Chapter Eleven

Everyone got an early start Sunday morning. Delaney sat at the breakfast nook nursing her second cup of coffee and watched Dario and his sister with amusement.

"Is my outfit too casual?" Maria Sofia asked as she hopped on one foot while she zipped up an ankle boot on the other.

Delaney studied how put-together the girl looked in her skinny jeans, snowy shirt and cherry-red blazer. She'd draped a scarf artfully around her shoulders. "Since the cat seems to have Dario's tongue," Delaney said, "I think you look fantastic."

"Thanks."

Dario set his cup in the sink. "Where's the laptop? You should be prepared to show other bulls in case a client loses interest in the first bull he asked about."

"I have it." His sister patted the carry-on she'd just set atop her wheeled case.

"Do you have your ticket and your passport?"

"Will you stop fussing? I have everything. I'll print the ticket at the airport. But we should go if we're dropping Delaney off at the hospital."

When the pair whirled toward her, Delaney waved an idle hand. "It's too early for visiting hours. I'll walk over later, so you can stay at the airport and see Maria Sofia off."

The girl rolled her eyes. "Joy, oh joy. He can give me fifty more lectures on the way."

Dario looked affronted. "You are still very young. Plus, Vicente reminded me at least a dozen times that it's my fault it's taken us half a decade to rebuild trade among US rodeo stockbrokers."

"I'm almost nineteen."

Delaney held her tongue until Dario had dug out his car keys. "I'm sorry your brother blames my dad, and me by association, for what went wrong five years ago."

Dario scrubbed a hand over his face. "Whatever happened, it *was* equivalent to the *estancia* being blackballed here in the United States."

"Delaney said she had no idea about that," Maria Sofia said. "Vicente should stop holding a grudge."

"Well, he's poisoned Papa's mind, too. It's time it all stops."

"Good luck with that. Papa's like a pit bull. Let's go, Dario. It won't help matters at home if I'm late and miss the plane."

They went out still bickering. Suddenly Dario stuck his head back into the kitchen. "I'll see you when I get back. I'd like us to have another talk."

Delaney clutched her cup more tightly. They kept dancing around their custodial situation. She simply could not face the thought of sending her son into the Sanchez lion's den. Dario wouldn't see how detrimental it'd be if his dad and brother ignored Nick, or worse, treated him like an outcast. Nick was so trusting. He didn't know how to be wary of anyone. Her worst fear was that Nick would be excited to go with Dario.

She dumped her coffee and went in to take a shower, hoping spray would wash away her anxiety.

IT WAS AFTER three when Dario blithely waltzed into Nick's ward, giving no explanation for why he'd been gone all day. Nick had fussed all morning, wanting his Daddy Dayo. Delaney had sent him a text, asking that he call to chat with Nick. She was frazzled and irritated that Dario hadn't bothered to check in.

"Daddy Dayo," the boy squealed. "I thought you went away and left me again."

The man lifted the boy out of bed and sat him on his lap. Frowning at Delaney, he said, "Didn't your mom tell you I took Tía to the airport?"

"I told him that at nine o'clock. It's after three."

Ignoring her barb, he spoke to Nick. "Where are the other kids? I figured you'd be having a good time playing with your friends."

"They're not here."

"Why not?"

"Some gots treatments. Some gots ther...thera... what's it called, Mommy?"

"Therapy. Dr. Von Claus cut Nick's experimental medicine. Maybe too much. I'm going to the break room for coffee. I'll ask the nurse." She headed for the door.

"I made us dinner reservations." Dario dropped the name of a pricey steak house on the River Walk.

Wavering, Delaney turned, her jaw dropping.

"How long since you've had an evening out with candlelight and wine?"

"Me, too?" Nick patted Dario's face.

"Only big people, champ. You'll be fast sleep by then."

The boy giggled and stretched up to kiss his dad's chin.

In spite of her weariness, Delaney felt the knots in her stomach loosening. It would be so easy to let anger and resentment drag her down. But she would accept his peace offering. "It's been too long, and your offer sounds heavenly. Can I bring you back something to drink?" she said, softening. "Nick, my little cowboy, I think I hear the break cart. Would you like chocolate pudding?"

"Uh-huh. Please. Then me 'n' Daddy Dayo can go to the room where Mike said they gots a train."

"*Have* a train. It's in the adjacent wing," Delaney said in response to Dario's arched eyebrow. "Mike told him about it at breakfast. Nick's very anxious for you to take him."

"Sure. We'll all go after snack."

"Nuh-uh, Mike says trains are just for boys."

"Not true, Nick. Girls, especially moms, can do all the stuff guys can do. That includes drive trains, fly planes or go into space. Remember that, okay?"

Wide-eyed, Nick bobbed his head.

Delaney couldn't help smiling. "You boys go ahead," she told them as she left. She wouldn't intrude on their outing. The difference in Nick's behavior, now that Dario was here, blew her mind. She'd once been told by a nurse that sick kids do better with both parents around, because a united family gave kids an added sense of security, which helped in the healing process.

Witnessing for herself the marked change in Nick literally moments after his dad had walked in, Delaney felt her resistance toward sharing Nick with Dario beginning to unravel. Some of her fears were still valid. Papa Sanchez and Vicente were determined to shake any hold they were certain she had on Dario—which was his situation to resolve.

Her new attitude made the day easier to deal with. She took a relaxing walk around the grounds while they went to see the trains.

When Delaney returned to the hospital room, Nick came back babbling excitedly. "Mommy, Mommy, that train is big and it runs all around the room, 'cluding around the ceiling."

"Cool. I saw a duck family swimming in a pond in one of the courtyards," Delaney told him. To Dario, she said, "Some families brought their children out in wheelchairs. Now that it's cooling off, I wonder if Dr. Von Claus would let Nick go outside if we bundled him up and put a mask on him."

"Why a mask?" Dario asked.

"The treatments can weaken his immune system. Speaking of which, Nick, Dr. Von Claus has changed you from pills to treatments. As soon as orderlies bring Mike and Richard back, it's your turn."

"Is that with needles that hurt?" His voice quivered.

"No, honey, it looks like an X-ray machine, remember?"

"Uh-huh. I hafta lay real still. I want Daddy Dayo to go with me."

"Oh, I don't know, buddy. That's something your mom handles."

Nick's lower lip trembled, and he grabbed hold of his dad's hand.

Delaney picked up the magazine she'd been reading. "Go with him today, Dario. You can't actually go in, but there's a waiting room. They even have puzzles set up for people to work on while they wait."

"Are you sure?" Dario cocked his head. "Not that I don't want to learn all I can about his routine, but…"

"It's okay." She cut him off. "I need to call the vets who are covering my practice anyway. I tried earlier, but both of their voice mails said they were out on calls."

"You've been away from your practice a long time. Might they want to buy you out?"

She shrugged. "I hope not. I do know one of the two would like to expand. His stepson is about to graduate from the same veterinary medicine program I attended. Their practice is a town away from La Mesa, but with the extended drought, and a third vet joining them…"

"You're pretty blasé."

"I don't have a choice, Dario."

It was good the orderlies came in, interrupting them. The boys they brought back chatted with Nick, who told them all about his trip to see the train.

Delaney relaxed again after Nick settled in the wheelchair and went to Radiology with Dario trailing along.

Delaney stepped out to call the other vets. Everything sounded fine, so she sat beside Nick's bed with a magazine. Not long after, two orderlies brought Heather into the ward, and a nurse came in to pull curtains around the girl's bed. After the nurse left,

Delaney heard the little girl crying quietly. "Heather, it's Nick's mom. Do you need help?"

"No. I'm okay. They're getting me ready to have a marrow transplant. They doubled my radiation. I guess I'm kinda scared. Dr. Von Claus wants my mom to come, but she may not be able to."

"I'm sorry, honey. I'm sure she'll try to be here. Nick went for a treatment. Is your stomach upset?"

"Yes. I can't play with the other kids today 'cause I might throw up."

"You can still talk to them." Delaney's heart felt heavy. Heather was almost seven. Here she'd been grousing about sharing Nick with Dario. Heather would give a lot to have family here. Delaney felt ashamed. "I'll keep checking on you, Heather."

"Okay." The sniffles slowly abated.

"The boys are watching a cartoon on TV. Would you like the curtain pulled back enough so you can see the show?"

"Yes, please."

Delaney rose and donned a mask from the disposable box hanging at the foot of Heather's bed. She knew when they started irradiating the whole body with high dose radiation prior to transplant it left a child extra vulnerable to germs. She tugged the curtains just wide enough apart for the girl to look over the foot of her bed. Heather thanked her in a small, squeaky voice.

She was removing the mask when the orderly pushed a wheelchair through the door. It took Delaney aback to see Dario riding in the chair, holding Nick against his chest.

Dario murmured, "He fell asleep during his treatment."

She nodded as Dario struggled to stand without jarring his burden. Nick looked so sweet and trusting, his head tucked into the crook of his father's neck. Delaney again felt muddled. Heather had no one, and Nick was surrounded by people who loved him.

Dario laid the boy in his bed and stood quietly gazing down on him while Delaney found his stuffed cow and tucked it in with him. "Is this normal?" Dario asked.

"Yes. He gets overly anxious because of the big machines, so he falls asleep. If he's zonked, the nurses may or may not wake him for dinner."

Dario glanced at his watch. "Are you comfortable leaving him? If so, we can go get ready for our dinner date."

"Yes. Heather," Delaney said, leaning close to the little girl's curtain, "if Nick wakes up and asks for us, would you mind telling him we'll be back in the morning?"

"Sure. Can you ask the nurses to come talk to me? I want to know if my mom is coming tomorrow."

"Of course, honey." Delaney explained the girl's situation to Dario once they were out of earshot.

"Poor little tyke," he said. "How soon after a transplant before she can go home?"

"Soon, I imagine. She'll need regular checkups for a year, and then they'll taper off. I feel so bad for her not having family here. I said I'd keep tabs on her." Delaney stopped at the nursing station to deliver Heather's message, then fell silent on the trek to the car.

"I didn't tell you I had a text from Maria Sofia.

She's already closed two sales in Chickasha. If she can close the deal in New Mexico, she'll grab an early flight back. She's so full of herself there'll be no living with her."

"But you're proud of her all the same?"

"Yeah." He pulled a wry face. "But I thought we'd have a few days to ourselves."

Delaney twisted her hands in her lap. "I know you want us to talk, Dario, and I've been stonewalling." She lowered her eyes and made a conscious effort to untangle her fingers as Dario swung into the driveway of their rental house. "I know it's time. Nick has given you his heart."

Dario slammed on the brakes. "Let's go inside. You have to tell me what has you so upset that even your voice is shaking."

They entered through the kitchen. Delaney paced until Dario blocked her path and took her in his arms. "Tell me the problem."

"It's the idea of having to send him away for half of every year, Dario. Schedule who gets Nick for which holiday or summer break. Next year kindergarten is only half a day, but the following year he'll spend a full day at school. Your seasons are different. Is your school year? That could be a problem. Frankly the very thought of putting him on a plane, trusting airline personnel to get him from Texas to Buenos Aires and back again until he's old enough to travel alone makes me physically ill."

He tightened his hold on her, setting his lips on her forehead. "You could fly with him."

"Easy for you to say. But I've already missed so

much work. And it's not like large animal vets make a ton of money." She sighed deeply.

He kissed her on the mouth then, a kiss that was surprisingly soft, yet thorough. Eventually he spoke against her lips, "I can't believe that's been festering inside you all this time. I have some news I want to share, but I want to do it over a nice evening out. Do you want to change clothes? You don't need to get fancy for a Western steak place."

"Good, the only dress I have with me is the sundress I wore when I visited your *estancia.*"

He leaned away from her, his eyes bright. "I only remember how it looked when you climbed up on Dancer behind Maria Sofia. That left an indelible impression."

She pretended to punch his chest. "I recall it rode up to my waist. You are such a…a…man."

His grin was unrepentant.

"Okay, we'll put our talk on hold. I'll only be a minute to get ready," she said, pulling free of his arms to leave the kitchen.

She was already in her room when she heard his cell phone ring. He called, "Delaney, it's Dr. Von Claus."

Delaney broke records getting back to the hall, where he stood with the phone at his ear. Why would Dr. Von Claus call Dario and not her?

Before she could check her phone, she noticed Dario's face had gone pale.

"You're sure?" he said. "There's no chance this is a mistake, or a clerical error?" The longer he listened, the more anxious Delaney grew. At last he said, "Thanks," and clicked off, at the same time blindly reaching out to her.

"What? What is it, Dario?" She grasped his hand.

"My tests are back. I'm…I'm…not a match."

His chest heaved, and Delaney felt his pain, remembering her own feelings when she got the same news. She wrapped him in her arms. "I'm sorry. I'm sorry. So sorry. Sorrier than you know."

"He said I have one more marker than you, but that's not close enough."

She stretched upward, aiming a kiss at his chin, but didn't quite reach and the kiss landed on his Adam's apple. His eyes were closed, but even in the dim light she saw his tears. She tightened her hold as dread raced through her.

He picked her up, squeezing her tight. "I wanted to help him. Wanted to be the match he needs. The doctor said Lorenzo also wasn't a match. What will we do now? What?"

"We'll keep trying. We'll hold another donor recruitment. I know how it hurts, Dario. Let's just stay in tonight."

"Thank you. I can't go out now," he said. "I want to howl at the moon." He loosened his hold, but Delaney sensed how badly he needed the connection. Attempting to comfort him, she wrapped her legs around his waist.

Dario held the back of her head and rained kisses on her face. She didn't know when their combined despair turned to physical desire, but soon he staggered the short distance to his dark bedroom and fell with her across the huge bed. The atmosphere around them felt heavy.

In the moment all Delaney could think of was easing a pain that never seemed to abate. It had been so long since she allowed herself to take solace from anyone. And this was the man she loved. The only man she'd ever loved. It seemed right that in this moment of dashed hope they could offer each other comfort skin to skin, body to body.

She was an equal participant in helping strip Dario of his clothing while he tore a few buttons off her gauzy blouse. Moonlight slid between the drapes.

Delaney laid a row of kisses up the center of his hot chest, and gloried in the slide of her bare thighs against his. She lay back and quivered with need, wanting him to ease an ache coiled deep inside her. Dario loomed over her on muscled arms, panting hard, but not moving. She could see the strain in his face and made herself ask, "What?"

"That's my question," he growled. "What are we doing? Last time I used protection and you still got pregnant. Tonight I'm here with nothing. This isn't right, Delaney. We can't use blind passion to try to rid ourselves of this pain."

The disappointment coursing through her, brought her back down from the peak she'd hit. She knew it was true. They couldn't afford to be careless again. She slid out from under him and hugged a pillow, feeling very vulnerable. "You're right. I let myself get carried away. I'll go. Don't forget to cancel our dinner reservations."

Glad for the shadows, she went to swing off the bed.

Dario stopped her. "I really don't want to be alone tonight. If I give you my word to behave, will you share my bed and just let me hold you close?"

Lord help her, she wanted more, but she'd settle for

sleeping in his arms. It seemed crazy for someone as controlled as she normally was. Refusing to examine her reasons too closely, she simply said, "I accept."

Chapter Twelve

Dario was jerked out of sleep by his phone ringing somewhere nearby. It was still dark, and for a moment he was confused. Why was his right arm held down? Then he remembered. Delaney, looking sleepy, sat up and began to collect her scattered clothing.

Ignoring the phone, Dario took a moment to stare. He loved how Delaney looked in simple pink underwear.

When she pulled on her jeans, he took her wrist. Simultaneously he managed to hit the talk button on his phone. "Hello? Oh…Maria Sofia? What time is it where you are?"

"I'm in Albuquerque."

"Ah, an hour earlier there." Dario stifled a yawn.

"Stop yammering and listen to me, Dayo. Yesterday I sold three bulls to the stock contractor here. Yay, yay and yay for me. But…as I checked out of my hotel a few minutes ago, I received a call from a lab at Nick's hospital. I'm a match, Dario. *A marrow match*," she shouted.

"You're a match?" He sat up and swung his legs off the bed. "When were you tested? Why didn't you tell us? I found out last night that I'm not a match. God, the fact you are is fantastic." Dario reached around and tugged Delaney closer.

She tried to talk, but he waved a hand to shush her.

Maria Sofia's voice got louder. "Is that Delaney? Are you guys already at the hospital? Oh, hey…did I interrupt something more, you sly dog?"

Dario ignored that. "Tell me everything," he said.

"Well, I was tested not too long after you. The day I met Nickolas."

"But how are you a match when I'm not? We're stepsiblings."

"The lab tech said my mom's ancestors might be similar to Delaney's, and you and I share Papa's ancestry with Nick."

Delaney was silent, but she pressed her head close to hear all that Maria Sofia was saying.

"It's not all good news, though, Dayo. I had to phone Vicente about the extra sales, but I got Papa. It's awful. He's furious at you for letting me go to sell the bulls. He's so angry he's canceling our *estancia* debit and credit cards, and he ordered me home straightaway. He didn't budge even after I explained that I can't leave because I'm the best donor for Nick. Papa says he won't allow me to donate. Can he do that? Oh, Dario, I'm sorry I've made a mess of everything."

Dario groaned. "Why would you call Vicente about the bulls? He would've gone straight to Papa."

"The stockman wanted to buy two bulls he saw on our website, but Vicente hadn't sent those stats. I needed him to prepare all the bulls I sold for shipment. And okay, I wanted to crow, too. But Papa was in the office. I thought he'd dance on the ceiling to hear I sold five bulls. Me! Five! That's a lot of money,

Dario. He commenced yelling, so I thought I'd better tell him I can't go home because of Nick. I thought he'd understand. That made things worse. I've never heard him be so furious."

"You know how he feels," Dario said. "Of course he's like a bull who saw red. He thinks you should take advanced piano lessons and do charity work."

"If he hasn't called yet to say he's disinheriting you, he will. Hey, I called and booked an earlier flight. The cab is dropping me at the airport. It's good I brought some cash. Listen, I land in San Antonio at ten fifty-five. Can you pick me up?"

"We'll be there."

"*Bueno*. Then will you call and straighten Papa out, please? We can't let him stop me from being Nick's marrow donor. And get him or Vicente to uncancel our bank cards, too."

"Honestly, I don't think Papa has any legal control over you now, but I'll find out." As it turned out she'd already hung up. He glowered at the phone, then tossed it aside.

"You're upset, I know. But, wow, she's a match!" Delaney's voice hit a high note. "Do you know what that means?"

Neither of them had gotten fully undressed, and Delaney jumped off the bed and danced around the room.

"Do you really know how upset I am?" Dario frowned. "If Papa can, he'll stop Maria Sofia."

Pausing, Delaney exhaled. "I'm going to head for the hospital. Dr. Von Claus and his team will be starting to make plans. They'll know the rules around age of consent. I don't think the lab would have tested her if she wasn't eligible. I'm walking on air, Dario. This is the break we've been waiting for."

"Wait," he called, and she stopped at the door. "I have plans I didn't get around to sharing with you last night."

"What plans? Besides owing me a dinner," she teased. Her mood had skyrocketed.

"A week ago I applied for a job. In Texas. To a firm on the cutting edge of wind and solar energy."

SHOCK MUST HAVE shown on her face, because Dario propelled himself off the bed. "Yesterday when I was gone so long, I drove up the freeway to check out one of their operations. The company plans to set up another wind farm on the high plains not far from your home. The owners are interested in my environmental studies degree and some of my wind projects on the *estancia*. They're considering me for the job. It's perfect, because I don't want to leave you and Nickolas."

She couldn't bring herself to speak, and his smile faltered. "This is where you tell me you want me to stay," he prompted.

"Are you saying…?" Delaney clutched the shoes she'd scooped up to her chest. "I can't process so much news at one time. I'm still high on knowing Maria Sofia can give Nick his one-in-a-million shot at permanent remission. And I'm panicking that your father could snatch that hope away. Do you think for a minute he'd let Nick and me lure you away from Estancia Sanchez?"

Catching hold of her shoulders, Dario yanked her close, bent his head and kissed her hard enough to take her breath away. Her brain whirled as ever so slowly he lifted his lips and gave her a smile that made her spine tingle.

"Okay, that's persuasive." She dropped her shoes and dragged his head down for another kiss. When it ended, she said with feeling, "Stay! For me and for our son."

Dario's phone buzzed again. Figuring it was his father or brother, Delaney dashed off to shower and give him privacy—although some part of her would have liked to listen in on that call.

GRIM AS HE looked when they later met in the kitchen for coffee, Delaney could tell his call hadn't been good.

"Papa is going to call Dr. Von Claus and forbid him from allowing Maria Sofia to donate. Then he swore to disinherit me, and he hung up. I called the local donor registry. The clerk said any individual who is eighteen and legally able to give informed consent can donate."

"I wonder if that's strictly United States. What do you suppose it means to be able to give informed consent?"

"I think it means being of sound mind and body."

"But what's the legal age for consent in your country? If it's twenty-one, we're sunk." Delaney poured coffee into their travel cups and shut off the pot.

"It's not twenty-one. In fact it's much younger for marriage and drinking. I suppose a local judge could support Papa's old-fashioned paternalistic ideas. He's completely old-world. Women are to be pampered but kept out of business, et cetera. What's odd is…right after Papa's call, I heard from Vicente. He surprised the heck out of me. He's all about profits and couldn't be happier with how Maria Sofia handled those sales.

Already the *estancia* has been wired down payments
from the stock contractors she saw. Vicente is happy
to give our sister Lorenzo and Marco's job. He even
said he'd unblock our debit and credit cards."

"That's wonderful for Maria Sofia. But, Dario, I
hate the thought of the rift the marrow donation is
causing in your family. At the same time I'm terrified
Maria Sofia might back out if your father threatens to
disown her. She's young, and that's a lot of pressure."

Dario hugged her, and Delaney set down the cups
to slide her arms around his waist. "I wish I could
wave a magic wand," he said, kissing her. "But really, what can he actually do from so far away? Hey,
if you're ready, let's go on to the hospital and see what
happens next."

"I do feel awful, Dario. I've been so afraid of sharing Nick with you. I haven't been fully on your side,"
she stammered as they left the house and she watched
him lock up.

"From the time I got here, I felt you saw me as
necessary but also a wolf at your door. I didn't understand at first."

They got in the car, and she said gravely, "Since
the day you came, I worried myself sick over the pos-
sibility of losing Nickolas. Not to cancer, but to you.
Up to then it'd been the two of us fighting medical
odds. Then he championed you. I…uh…consulted a
legal adviser who said I opened the door for joint custody when I listed you as the father on Nick's birth
certificate."

Dario had started the car, but he still reached for
her hand. "That gives me hope like nothing else that
we still have a future, Delaney. We let our fathers and

circumstance drive us apart. But I'm still single be-cause I measure every woman I meet against you."

"Dario, that's the nicest compliment anyone's ever paid me."

HALF AN HOUR later at the hospital, a nurse caught them as they passed her station. "Dr. Von Claus and Dr. Mc-Crory, the marrow transplant specialist, have sched-uled a meeting with all of you for this afternoon at three. Everyone's thrilled that Ms. Sanchez is a match." A light flashed outside a room down the hall. She smiled before scurrying away.

"They aren't wasting any time," Dario said.

"Dario, if I wanted to make a short video to try and appeal to your dad, is there anyone at the *estancia* who would make sure he sees it?"

"Lorenzo. But Papa may not view it. He's a stub-born old goat. Vicente said Papa deleted any of the photos I emailed them of Nickolas."

"Can I have Lorenzo's email address anyway? For Nick's sake and ours, I have to try to convince him how awful it'd be to try and stop Maria Sofia from donating marrow. She needs focus, not to be upset."

"I'm pretty sure she won't cave, but I'll find out for sure when I pick her up at the airport."

"He is her father, her only parent," Delaney said. "Let's go see Nick. I'll take photos of you two with my phone. I'm sure the computer at home has basic video editing software, and I can email everything to your brother."

"Go for it. Here's Lorenzo's card. Don't forget I need to go to the airport in an hour to meet Maria Sofia."

"It won't take me that long. I intend to keep my plea short. Would you like to preview it once I pull stuff together?"

"I trust you." He punctuated his declaration with a kiss.

She grew teary and clutched his arm. "So much time wasted when we could have been a family."

"We'll make it happen," he promised.

As they entered the ward, Nick was noticeably fidgety. "Where have you guys been? Heather had to go to another room so she can get 'pared for bone marrow."

"Prepared," Delaney corrected. She nudged Dario's arm to get his attention. Obviously Nick hadn't heard yet that he, too, had a match. "We should wait to tell him until we're sure about Maria Sofia," she murmured so Nick couldn't hear.

With a nod, Dario took out the iPad he'd left in Nick's nightstand. "Want to play a game, champ? Your mom needs a few minutes to go do something. When she comes back, I'm running out to pick Tía up at the airport."

"Did she sell some bulls?"

"Did she ever. I'll let her tell you all about it." Dario pulled a chair close to the bed and glanced up as Delaney snapped a few photos.

BACK AT THE RENTAL, Delaney agonized over how to caption her photos. Finding it impossible to put her plea for the elder Sanchez's forbearance into words, she decided to phone Lorenzo to see if Dario's brother had any ideas.

The phone rang twice before a man answered.

"Lorenzo Sanchez?" Delaney queried.

"Yes. Who is this?"

"Delaney Blair. Listen, please don't hang up." She quickly outlined what she planned to do and what she hoped to accomplish.

"Uh, hold on."

Minutes ticked past, and had Delaney not heard noise in the background, she would have thought he'd hung up.

"I'm here, but I don't have long. I'm escorting Papa to San Antonio."

"What?"

"We're in Miami. I was about to call Dayo. Our flight lands in San Antonio at one forty-five."

"Oh, wow. Your father's making the trip on such short notice and in his condition?"

"He's fine. He's tough. Sorry to cut you off, but I have to call Dayo to let him know."

"Sure. No. I mean, don't call him, please. I'll come for you. It's my best hope of convincing your father that I'm not an ogre. And Nickolas is a sweet, inno-cent boy. It may have no impact, but I've got to try."

"I guess," the man mumbled. "Okay. We're on flight 1251. You have red hair, right?"

"And freckles. I'll be in jeans and a blue shirt. I look harmless. I am harmless."

"Gotta go," he said, and he hung up.

Sweating, Delaney rose and poured a glass of water. What had she done? Dario said he trusted her. How wrong was it to keep quiet about this? Wrong, but she'd already set her course. Now she really had to figure out what to say, and make her words count. Yikes, she needed to get back to the hospital so Dario could fetch Maria Sofia. Delaney had a vision of what might happen if one plane was early and the other late. Lordy, they could have a showdown in the middle of baggage claims.

Delaney parked and hurried into the hospital to return Dario's car keys. She'd also have to walk back to the house for her vehicle.

Dario rose and greeted her as she stepped into the ward. "Good, you're back," he said. "I'm leaving my laptop with Nick. He's watching a cartoon. I wish I had time to hear how your project went, but fill me in when I'm back. See you in an hour or so."

Relief coursed through her, followed by waves of guilt. She loved Dario so much. Add that to loving Nick with all her heart, and she knew she was following the true compass of her heart. She sat with him for an hour to watch his cartoon, then hugged him tight. "Daddy Dayo will be back soon, my little cowboy. Mommy needs to run an errand."

"My cartoon's over. Can't you stay?"

"For a minute. But I need you to tell Daddy Dayo I'll be back in time for a meeting with your doctor."

"He's bringing Tía. She sold a bunch'a bulls."

"That's right. Oh, look, Mike's back from therapy. Maybe you guys can build something with Legos. I want to run home, change clothes, and I need to pick up my car for the errand I mentioned."

She led Nick to the play table and left the boys sorting through colorful blocks.

As SHE LUCKED into a coveted ground-floor parking spot at the busy airport, Delaney thought she'd only ever been this nervous three times before. Twice when doctors told her Nick had leukemia. The third time nerves got the best of her—on the flight to face Dario with the news he was a father.

She reached the baggage area and checked the reader board for the flight number about the time people streamed off a flight. She'd cut it close, and worried that she might have missed them when she saw a younger version of Dario step out of an elevator. He assisted a stern-faced older man seated in a wheelchair. People surged around them toward baggage carousels. Delaney held her purse strap more tightly and wiped her damp, free hand down her thigh. She lifted her chin and strode toward the men.

"Lorenzo," she said, tilting a smile his way.

He grinned. "Delaney Blair, I presume. Papa, this is…"

"I heard." The man in the chair sneered. He followed that with some sharp words in Spanish that Delaney didn't know, but his tone wasn't kind.

She plopped down cross-legged in front of his chair. "While your son gets your bags, I have a few things I need to say. I trust you will hear me out. Dario has said many times you're a gentleman. A defender of women." Her voice was soft and polite. Her smile felt welded in place. Thankfully Arturo Sanchez didn't try to power over her in his wheelchair. "I know you came here to stop Maria Sofia from donating marrow to your grandson. Your only grandson," she stressed. "I have no family left except for Nickolas. I brought along photos of him with Dario." She punched up the pictures she'd taken only hours before and held the first one in front of the old man's face. "You can see how much of a Sanchez Nick is." She eased back a bit, so he didn't have to cross his eyes.

Arturo remained mute. Delaney scrolled to the second shot. "Aren't they two peas in a pod?"

Lifting a gnarled hand, the man took the phone. He ran his other hand over his face in a gesture Delaney found reminiscent of Dario. "Nick would benefit from the wisdom of a grandfather," she said, and waited.

Lorenzo plodded back, wheeling one bag, with a duffle slung over his shoulder. He seemed shocked to see Delaney still there. And more shocked when his father thrust the phone toward him. "Your brother has done his part to carry on the family legacy. You and Vicente could take a few lessons," he said gruffly.

Delaney covered a smile with her hand, but sobered the minute she saw the old man's cold eyes. "Where is Dario that he sent a woman to pick a man's fight? Oh, but then he sent his baby sister off to talk bulls with strange men." He added a string of rapid-fire Spanish.

Vaulting up, Delaney took her phone from Lorenzo. "Dario doesn't know I'm here, or that you're here. And I don't think it's any secret that you've raised a headstrong, competent daughter, Mr. Sanchez."

Arturo laughed a rusty laugh and slapped the plaid robe that covered his injured legs. This time his string of Spanish sounded more jovial.

Leaning in, Lorenzo murmured, "He said you have the grit of his sons' mother, and the creative shrewdness of our sister's mother." He flashed Delaney a thumbs-up.

"I parked on the ground floor, right across from this door," she said, pointing to the exit. "I can drive you to your hotel, but after dropping you off I have to leave for a meeting with Nickolas's doctors."

"No hotel," Arturo growled, and continued in a mix

of English and Spanish. "Vicente said Dario and Maria Sofia rented a big hacienda. *Sí,* Lorenzo? We'll save *mucho dinero* and *la familia* will be under one roof. And…I will attend *el mitin, sí.*"

"Madre mía," Lorenzo muttered. "He wants to attend the meeting."

Delaney's head pounded. She wondered if she could fake a flat tire and miss the meeting. This wasn't entirely her mess, but she still should not have hidden Arturo's arrival from Dario. "We can run by our house and drop your things."

"You live there, too?" Lorenzo asked, tossing the bags in the back before helping his father into the front passenger seat.

"I rent with them, yes," she said. Lorenzo folded the chair and wedged it into the backseat, then climbed in after it. As they drove, the men conversed in Spanish. She thought they were comparing San Antonio to Buenos Aires, but they spoke too fast for her to follow.

After the brief stop by the house to off-load bags, they arrived at the hospital. Due to good, or bad, fortune they parked directly behind Dario's rental car. It still hung over her head that, in keeping his father's arrival a secret, she could have ruined the progress she'd made with Dario over the past two days.

With heavy heart and dread, Delaney watched Lorenzo unload and set up his father's wheelchair. She went to turn her phone off for the meeting and saw it was already in silent mode. She had three missed calls from Dario and one from Maria Sofia. *Hooboy!* "Ready?" she asked, forcing a smile.

After stopping at the main reception desk to get visitor badges for Arturo and Lorenzo, he fell in be-

hind Delaney, wheeling his father as they went to Dr.
Von Claus's office on the third floor. Arriving at two
minutes to three, they found two doctors, Dario and
Maria Sofia already in the room. Delaney could see
them through the loosely woven curtains covering the
inner windows. When she nudged open the door, Dario
exploded out of his chair. "Where on earth have you
been? I've been worried sick."

Opening the door wider, Delaney sidled in. "I've
brought guests."

Using his hands, Arturo rolled himself into the
room followed by Lorenzo.

Dario's mouth dropped open. *"Que lío!"*

"Papa…Lorenzo," Maria Sofia squealed. She sprang
out of her seat.

The doctors at the head of a rectangular table half
rose. Dr. Von Claus stretched out a hand to the elder
Sanchez. "Welcome. I'm Dr. Von Claus, the lead on
Nickolas's team. This is Dr. McCrory, the team's marrow transplant specialist. We could not be more delighted that a member of Nick's family has near-perfect
markers. This meeting is to lay out a time line and answer questions. Wait, do you speak English?"

"Enough. I did not consent to have my only daughter leeched like a guinea pig," Arturo said in labored
English.

Dr. McCrory scanned several papers he held. "We
understand some parents do express concern. However, she's of legal age to consent to this procedure."
He made eye contact with Arturo. "My assistant examined Ms. Sanchez's last physical exam and found
her to be in excellent health. We have booklets outlin-
ing the entire process." He handed a binder to Maria

Sofia, and passed one to Delaney, and gave the last one to Arturo. "This meeting is strictly informational."

"I'm doing this, Papa," Maria Sofia said. "I keep telling you I don't want to be coddled. And after I do this for my nephew, I want to keep working for the *estancia*. I love ranching. I love marketing. I hate going to stuffy museum fund-raisers And I play a miserable piano. With Dayo leaving the *estancia* to move here, I want to be a full partner in the business."

Delaney flinched, seeing that came as a total bomb-shell to both Arturo and Lorenzo. The older man's work-roughened hands plucked at his robe. Silence fell, which made the elder Sanchez's next statement seem louder and more forceful. "Senorita Blair showed me photos of Nickolas. He's Sanchez. He is my grand-son. So, I will remain in San Antonio through all pro-cedures. Once the boy is well enough to travel, his parents will bring him to the *estancia*. There we will make changes to the *familia* trust, giving Maria Sofia a partnership, and adding Nickolas. Following, there will be a proper Argentine wedding with a priest be-fore Dayo and his *familia* return to Texas. Until my last breath I still rule Estancia Sanchez." He pounded a fist on the arm of his wheelchair, and then again on the closed binder as if for emphasis. "I'm not happy, but for all these things I give my blessing."

Only Maria Sofia reacted. She flung her arms around her father and kissed his leathery cheek, fur-ther flustering the man. "I love you, Papa."

Delaney sneaked a glance at Dario, and her heart dipped. The smokiness she loved was gone from his eyes. They were now flinty. He looked angry. Had she made a mistake not telling him before bringing his family here?

The doctors routinely dealt with uncomfortable family issues. They wasted no time launching into how a marrow transplant worked. They covered every aspect before pausing to ask if Maria Sofia understood all that was involved on her part.

"I think so. Will this put Nick in permanent remission?"

Dr. Von Claus looked over his half glasses. "In this business I've learned never to make guarantees. But his chances are a hundred percent better than they were the day before your test results came back, young lady."

"That's good enough for me."

Delaney threw her arms around the girl in a bear hug. "Thank you. And, Mr. Sanchez, thank you." She wiped away her tears.

Dr. McCrory stood. "We'll let you tell Nick the good news. His prep and Ms. Sanchez's will begin tomorrow."

Arturo had to back his wheelchair out of the room before anyone else could leave. Dr. Von Claus fell into step beside him, with Lorenzo now pushing the chair. Dr. McCrory walked with Maria Sofia.

Delaney took Dario's elbow. "I knew they were in Texas before you went after Maria Sofia. I'm sorry I kept you in the dark. I was desperate to try and make your father see this wasn't about us banding against him, but all about saving Nick's life."

"No need for you to apologize. You succeeded, and I'm grateful for that."

"Yes, but I feel wretched that he continues to try and order your life."

"Me, too, but he'll never change."

"Still, he is your father, Dario. It took me a while to come to this, but I'd like Nick to learn about your family and your business. I'm willing to take him to the *estancia* to visit once he's well enough to travel. It may be up to a year, however. Please, believe me when I say the last thing I expect is for you to follow your dad's directive to marry me."

"You don't want to marry me?"

"I didn't say that. But we both know the harm meddling can cause. Look what happened with both our fathers."

Dario took her flailing hands and brought them to his chest. She could feel the thud of his heart. "I want to marry you. I intended to ask you properly. But, since Papa jumped the gun, will you do me the honor of becoming my wife?" He carried her hands to his lips and kissed her knuckles.

Delaney couldn't answer at first. Finally, she said, "I thought nothing could make me happier than finding out Nick had a donor. You just tied that, Dario. Can you hold the thought, though, until Nick's well enough to walk me down the aisle?"

"Absolutely. I love you, Delaney. I knew it when we met. I was too young and too foolish and I walked away."

"It's taken me time to admit why I named you on Nick's birth certificate. I couldn't let you go completely out of our lives. You have always owned my heart."

"Hey, slowpokes," Maria Sofia called. "I want to

tell Nick I'm his marrow match. Will it be too much excitement to let him meet his grandfather? Papa wishes to see him."

"Of course," Delaney said.

"What do you suppose those two will make of each other? Nick and Papa?" Dario murmured, placing a broad hand on Delaney's waist as they joined the others.

Her eyes gleamed wickedly. "My money's on Nick further melting your father's crusty heart."

"Yeah." Dario's rich laugh sent desire curling through Delaney.

Chapter Thirteen

Eighteen months later

After weathering a year of uneventful follow-ups, Nick was able to attend school for the first time, and he fit right in. Dario accepted the job with the wind and solar company, which he loved. Dario and Delaney didn't wait for Nick to be pronounced officially in remission before they visited a Justice of the Peace and were married in the eyes of Texas law—and themselves.

Six months later, during a school break, the three flew to Argentina as Arturo Sanchez had decreed. Nick loved the *estancia*. Everyone on the estate loved him. Consuelo did her best to fatten all of them up prior to the high-mass wedding. It made for a whirlwind couple of weeks.

At long last Delaney and Dario were in their kitchen in La Mesa putting the last touch of sprinkles on cupcakes Delaney had baked to take to Nick's first-grade class. Nick was about to turn six, and he told everyone he met.

His parents were walking on air because Dr. Avery, who'd handled Nick's checkups since his marrow transplant, had given him the long-awaited all-clear last week, which meant Maria Sofia's marrow had become his entirely.

"You have chocolate frosting on your face," Delaney said, swiping at the corner of Dario's mouth.

He started to lick it, then instead, bent and kissed her, mumbling against her lips that she should taste her handiwork, too.

Nick, taller by two inches and heavier by ten pounds than when he'd met his dad for the first time, entered the kitchen bouncing an ever-present soccer ball. He was followed by a poodle pup he had yet to name. It was a birthday gift from Dario, who remembered Nick saying way back in the hospital that he wanted a dog. Since infections and allergies were concerns for posttransplant kids, Dario had researched and chosen a poodle, a breed with very little dander.

"Grandpapa is on Skype," Nick announced. "Oh, cool, are those my birthday cupcakes?"

"They are." Delaney gave her new husband a final kiss and began placing the cupcakes in a box. It hadn't been a month since they'd had a small wedding anniversary barbecue at the Bannerman ranch.

"Who does Grandpapa Sanchez want to talk with?" Delaney asked.

"Daddy, even though I told him we got the tickets he sent to go visit over my school spring break. Is that when we getta go to Argentina again?"

"Week after next. How are you feeling?" Delaney turned from the counter and set a hand on Nick's forehead.

He ducked away. "Mom! How many times do I hafta say I feel good?"

"Indulge your mother." Dario spoke from the archway outside Nick's room. "She's earned the right to worry about the people she loves."

Delaney nodded. "I know you feel a lot better, honey. I also know there's huge potential for overexcitement, between your birthday party at school and Tía Maria Sofia arriving from Amarillo tonight."

"My birthday party at the restaurant is after we watch Zoey and Brandy's soccer team beat Lubbock, right?"

Dario laughed. "Will your party still be fun if their team loses?" He plucked the ball threatening to land in the cupcakes and slid his free arm around Delaney.

"They haven't lost yet this year," Nick bragged. "Zoey said my being at the games brings them good luck."

"No pressure," Delaney noted. "So, what did your dad want?" she asked Dario a few moments later.

"He wants you to have the mantilla my mother wore when they got married. The one he let you wear for our Argentine ceremony. I assumed he'd save it for Lorenzo's and Vicente's brides, but I said okay. Hey, hey, why the tears? Was I wrong?" he asked, drying her cheeks with his thumb.

"No, not at all." She pressed her mouth against the exposed skin at the V-neck of his T-shirt. "I get weepy every time I think about how far we've all come," she murmured.

Nick ran his finger around the frosting bowl. "I love my puppy, but Zoey's gonna have a baby brother or sister."

"What?" Delaney spun in his direction. "Jill and Mack are pregnant? Who said?"

Nick licked frosting off his finger and looked smug.

"Zoey told Brandy yesterday when I got to watch their soccer practice. It's maybe a secret. But, I said I'd sure like a brother. Or maybe a sister, if she liked soccer."

Dario crooked his forefinger under Delaney's chin and turned her toward him again. Smiling into her eyes with the heat of passion, he answered Nick, "I promise you, son, we're working on that. Oh, yeah… definitely working on it."

* * * * *